"Let Me Up."

"Do you hate all humans because of that one person?" he said, inflexible persistence in his voice.

"That's beneath answering. If I'd known you were going to grill me for breakfast, I'd have gone to another restaurant!"

His rich baritone chuckle infuriated her. Not bothering to hide her irritation, she asked, "Why are you pushing so hard, anyway?"

His devilish grin flashed. "Love me, love my dog. How can I expect to marry you until that's resolved?"

"You can't—on both counts," she stated firmly. "I thing you have bats in your belfry."

"And passion in my pa—"

"Watch it!"

He smiled with all the innocence of a street urchin. "I was only going to say 'in my palpitating heart.'"

Dear Reader:

Series and Spin-offs! Connecting characters and intriguing interconnections to make your head whirl.

In Joan Hohl's successful trilogy for Silhouette Desire— *Texas Gold* (7/86), *California Copper* (10/86), *Nevada Silver* (1/87)—Joan created a cast of characters that just wouldn't quit. You figure out how *Lady Ice* (5/87) connects. And in August, "J.B." demanded his own story—*One Tough Hombre*. In *Falcon's Flight*, coming in November, you'll learn *all* about . . .?

Annette Broadrick's *Return to Yesterday* (6/87) introduced Adam St. Clair. This August *Adam's Story* tells about the woman who saves his life—and teaches him a thing or two about love!

The six Branigan brothers appeared in Leslie Davis Guccione's *Bittersweet Harvest* (10/86) and *Still Waters* (5/87). September brings *Something in Common*, where the eldest of the strapping Irishmen finds love in unexpected places.

Midnight Rambler by Linda Barlow is in October—a special Halloween surprise, and totally unconnected to anything.

Keep an eye out for other Silhouette Desire favorites— Diana Palmer, Dixie Browning, Ann Major and Elizabeth Lowell, to name a few. You never know when secondary characters will insist on their own story. . . .

All the best,

Isabel Swift
Senior Editor & Editorial Coordinator
Silhouette Books

SELWYN MARIE YOUNG
Forever Mine

Silhouette Desire
Published by Silhouette Books New York
America's Publisher of Contemporary Romance

SILHOUETTE BOOKS
300 East 42nd St., New York, N.Y. 10017

Copyright © 1987 by Selwyn Young

ISBN: 0-373-05369-X

First Silhouette Books printing August 1987

America's Publisher of Contemporary Romance

Printed in the U.S.A.

SELWYN MARIE YOUNG

lives in Seattle, Washington, and works as a secretary for her architect husband, to whom she's been married for thirty-four years. They have eight children, for whom she wrote jingles, poems and short stories as they grew up. The author has always been interested in arts and crafts. After studying jewelry design, she was at one time involved in a working gallery every bit as eclectic and exciting as the one described in *Forever Mine*. She is a voracious romance reader as well as a writer, and an avowed romantic with a firm belief in love ever after.

To my husband, for the love and time I needed;
the crew, especially Mary and Annette,
who wouldn't take no for an answer;
Helen McGrath for believing; the Thursday group,
Pat, Shiela, Nancy and Betty, who laughed in all the
right places but never let me get away with a thing;
and Tara Hughes and Anne Leiner, editors
extraordinaire, without whom it wouldn't have
happened, with heartfelt thanks.

One

The day should have been ideal, Blair thought as she ran an unsteady hand over the tense spot at the nape of her neck. An August sun blazed in a sky so blue it almost hurt. Even at this altitude its heat had her T-shirt sticking to her back as she sat sprawled across the rough, narrow track, one jean-clad leg extended, the other serving as a prop for a set, dejected chin.

Her gaze dropped to her leg as she came to terms with two irrefutable truths: her reinjured "soccer knee" was assuming grapefruit-size proportions, and the fast-approaching darkness would be not only cold but long. Now, thanks to her less-than-graceful gallop across the rockfall, it threatened to be miserable to boot. It was not, she decided wryly, an auspicious beginning for a week of lazy hiking in the remote areas of Washington's High Cascades, a change of scenery she'd felt she needed.

Her summer had been hectic. A surprising number of tourists who'd flooded the Puget Sound basin had found

their way to her art gallery in Edmonds, just north of Seattle. Grinning from ear to ear, she and her partners had
worked like Trojans to keep their walls filled and the cash
register ringing, needing to fill the financial gap between
summer and their major fall show. But when even her
boundless energy had started to flag, the lure of some rest
and the pure air of wide-open spaces had been more than
tempting.

What had finally tipped the scales were voices from a past
she had considered long buried. Blair frowned. There was
no explanation she could think of for the spate of phone
calls she'd begun getting from Greg and her former mother-
in-law. Minor irritations, but ones she didn't have the patience to deal with at the moment. And what better place to
be out of reach of her ex-husband and Bea, she'd concluded, then halfway up the side of a mountain?

Which postponed one problem but landed her with another.

"Way to go, Mackenzie." Assessing her situation, Blair
impatiently ran her fingers through the short tumble of
mahogany curls that crowned her head. At least she had
supplies to last until she could work her way back down to
civilization, if she was careful. Careful, ha! Hindsighted
advice she wished she had heeded earlier. When would she
learn to look before she leaped?

"Well, you got yourself into this. Now get yourself out,"
she said firmly, and began mentally sorting through the
contents of her backpack, balancing what she had against
what she'd now need.

She swept her gaze over the thick undergrowth that covered the feet of the towering firs. The huckleberries, she
noted absently, would add interest to her dried-fruit mix
when she reached the point where she could even think
about a meal.

That they were also a tasty invitation to the local bear
population, she refused to consider. No hunter herself, she

had enough experience to be fairly confident the spoor she'd seen a hundred yards back was several days old. She hoped. At any rate, she'd be up and away at first light.

Meanwhile, her knee required attention before she could begin setting up some sort of camp.

The narrow trail wasn't exactly an ideal spot, Blair admitted. Beyond the boulder supporting her back, the ground dropped hundreds of feet to a wide meadow. If only she hadn't been so darn independent, she'd have been there, on level ground, set up, intact...and open to encroachment by other hikers.

Blair's jaw tightened. If-onlys. They had done nothing for her brief marriage and would do nothing for her now. She forced her gaze back to the throbbing lump under her jeans. "Perfect timing, you traitor. Thanks a heap."

The staccato words startled a jay into indignant flight. Small frantic noises from the underbrush made Blair's mouth curve in lopsided apology. "Sorry, guys." There was little comfort in knowing something was more disturbed than she.

Forcing reluctance out of her mind, she reached for her left pant leg. First things first.

Sometime later, her thin T-shirt damp with effort, Blair cast concerned eyes around the makeshift campsite. Its haphazard confusion was as upsetting to her well-ordered mind as the constant throb from her oddly wrapped knee. She was tempted to just swallow a couple of aspirins and roll into her sleeping bag, but training coupled with experience changed her mind. Even in the summer, Pacific Northwest nights were cold in the mountains, and rain always hovered at the edges of a forecast, so, like it or not, the tent had to go up.

"Pull yourself together, Blair. Survival's the name of the game."

Spoken aloud, the talisman helped. Heaven knew she'd tested the truth of that often enough.

Damn her trick knee. While she was at it, damn her decision to camp out. She grabbed a piece of wood. If she'd zipped off to Bermuda, the most she'd have risked would have been sunburn and bankruptcy.

Frustration fueled her arms and her good leg as she struggled upright. She adjusted herself into reasonable balance as she shifted her body, digging her right foot into the ground for purchase. The tree limb she'd found to use as a crutch not only dug itself into her armpit but was so supple that it bent alarmingly when she applied any weight. She was reduced to a precarious hop-shuffle, but at least she was mobile. So much for that, she decided. Get on with it.

A crash in the nearby bushes froze her in motion. Birds exploded into the air, screeching in alarm.

Oh, God. Blair swallowed hard. "Don't overreact, and don't *move*, Mackenzie!" Her whispered words fell into the ensuing eerie silence as if the intruder and she were both poised on a thin thread of impending circumstance.

Oh, help, what she couldn't give for X-ray eyes. She cringed at the pop of cracking twigs as an enormous shadow lumbered through the underbrush not twenty feet away. If she held still, she thought, it might go away—whatever it was.

But the primitive grunting, the dark menacing shape and size, linked in her mind with the spoor she'd seen on the trail. Even without a bad knee, she could never outrun a bear! Alternatives flashed through her head as she swayed, heart pounding, mesmerized by the sound of slashing claws tearing at bushes and coming closer.

Her heart dropped to her stomach as the greenery was ripped aside, ending all guesswork. Short-tempered black eyes held her rigid as the bear's scruffy brown-furred body swelled in outrage. Blair's feet were glued to the ground, her nostrils repelled by a pungent odor. Sweat broke out on her palms. What should she *do*?

Scare him! she thought, grasping at straws. That was it!

Blair opened her mouth to yell when a low, deadly snarl from behind her iced the blood in her veins. She whirled instinctively, to stare with horror into the glaring eyes of a black fangs-bared hound from the depths of hell.

Panic exploded in her mind and the sapling flew from her hold as she fought for balance, arms flapping ineffectually.

"Brutus! Protect!"

A demonic male voice launched the snarling monster straight for her throat. With a shriek of desperation, she threw herself sideward. Hips and shoulders hit rock first, then she both felt and heard her head crack against granite as everything was lost in gray enveloping fog.

Somewhere in the distance were a commanding voice and the sounds of a terrible scuffle. But she seemed to float up, away from it all. Superimposed on her eyelids was the impossible image of a . . . a plaid-shirted bear.

Too late a warning tolled in her brain. "Stay awake!" Her whole body shuddered as Blair grasped the blank relief offered by a dead faint.

Though her eyes remained closed, bits and pieces of recall held Blair rigid while, like a cornered animal, she used her senses to cautiously test her immediate surroundings. Fingers and spine confirmed she lay on some padded support. Although her head throbbed—with good reason; *that* she remembered—she felt warm, even comfortable, except for her knee, which seemed to be tightly bound in a cage of ice.

Strange. But no danger there. Did she *dare* open her eyes?

With a burst of courage, she risked a peek. Mere feet away from her face, a small campfire crackled with false cheer, the only sound disturbing the familiar stillness of the wilderness.

Or was it?

Her ears strained with concentration. There had been something . . .

There! She had caught . . . snuffling? A sighing, or a restless movement just outside her vision?

Fear coursed through her, raising gooseflesh and memories of childhood dreams. No! Her painful experience with animals—dogs—was buried in the past. She couldn't begin that again! Not after all this time. Defiantly, she snapped her eyes open.

Everything inside her congealed into icy realization. She was staring into the wicked face of the biggest, ugliest dog she'd ever seen—and it was staring back!

"Woof!" the black animal said.

Which catapulted her two feet into the air on the heels of a screech shrill enough to scrape bark from the trees. Her feet never touched the ground as she cleared the low fire in a blind bid for safety. She came down running and managed to take three steps before her knee buckled, pitching her forward.

Solid columns of undetermined origin caught her around the waist. The impact drove the breath from her lungs and folded her in half. Somewhere above her pretzeled body a deep-chested voice rose in a pungent curse.

That voice! The attacker! She was dead! she thought irrationally.

Thrusting herself upright, blind with terror, Blair fought, tore, scratched, to break free.

"Hey! Hold it! What's the matter with you? Are you nuts?"

"Let me go," she cried. Her fingers scrabbled at the huge hands locked around her middle.

And suddenly she *was* free, stumbling forward . . . on a dead line with that beast leaping toward her, thick lips curled back, baring teeth bloodred in the firelight.

Blair spun and leaped, burrowing deep into the strong arms that closed around her small frame and lifted her high in the air. She clutched at the imposing contours of male

shoulders as her legs clasped in a locking hold around a solid
waist. "Don't let him near me!"

Her voice held all the terror of her worst nightmares, as
she instinctively knew that the forces holding her firmly
against the broad chest was her only haven from hell.

"Brutus—" she felt more than heard the deep rumble
against her ear "—go lie down." The voice softened per-
ceptibly. "He won't hurt you, you know."

Not believing it for a minute, Blair dug herself further
into the warm safe arms of her captor. She buried her nose
under a wool shirt collar into the strong-corded comfort of
his neck. It was, she knew, like an ostrich skewering its head
in the sand, but at that moment she didn't care. One crisis
at a time.

It took some doing, but gradually her shudders sub-
sided, and as the large man shifted his weight, reality surfaced in her mind.

She was in the arms of a stranger, someone who, for reasons she couldn't remember at the moment, was a threat. A
plaid-shirted bear of a man whose scent, she realized with a
sense of shock, was a mixture of woodsmoke, pine and
other, elusive male elements that were strangely pleasing to
her scrambled senses. Her lips, pressed against the steady
pulse in the dip above his collarbone, bore the taste of saltiness from her tears and the tang of his skin. There was
inexhaustible strength in those arms, which still patiently
cradled her against the heated security of his upper body.
Her fingertips sent messages of the smooth flow of su-
perbly conditioned muscle, sinew, bone....

To her intense mortification she realized that ice pack and
all, her legs had a death grip around his waist. And, cring-
ing, she became aware of a bulky buckle cutting into the
sensitive softness of her thigh. Blair stiffened, face suf-
fused with heat from the swift shift in the emphasis of her
danger.

She *knew* he had sensed the tightening; she felt it the length and breadth of his upper body. She could only pray he didn't know why. She made her fingers relax their clutch and inched her flattened breasts away from the warm wall of his chest as his hands curved more firmly around her buttocks. Oh, my gosh, when had she...?

"Are you okay?" he asked.

She jolted, then calmed. The quiet resonance in his voice momentarily steadied the bizarre directions of her thoughts. "Y-yes, I'm fine. Let...me down, please." A sudden memory retightened her arms and legs. "Where...where is...?"

"Brutus? On the other side of the fire, sulking." She picked up the smile in his voice. "You've hurt his feelings."

"You must be joking!" Blair couldn't control the shudder that cracked her voice.

"Are you sure you're okay?"

This was no time for pride. "Is...it safe? He won't..."

"Lady, take a look at him. He's more frightened of and bewildered by your actions than you could ever be by his."

"Don't bet on it!" Blair snapped.

His huge hand soothed her from shoulder to hips, a menace to her concentration. "Trust me. He's a marshmallow."

"With a name like Brutus?" She kept her eyes on the finely stretched shirtfront, reluctant to raise her eyes past the dark wealth of his beard.

"He's such a pushover, he needed some clout."

She felt his laughter through her thighs and thought with some hysteria, How do I get out of this...?

Ask, you ninny! She ran the tip of her tongue over dry lips. "Please. Let me down."

"No hurry. Take your time."

Now she knew darned well that humor was aimed at her! Her eyes snapped upward and fell into the bottomless trap

of laughing gray eyes. His thick straight brows peaked with
amusement in a tanned face with bold features. His eyes, the
high prominent cheekbones, strong nose and full, surprisingly sensual mouth clearly defined by his thick facial
growth had her mouth almost dropping open.

Usually she didn't care for beards on men, suspecting they
were handy, fortunately stylish, methods of disguising weak
chins. In this case, she didn't think so for a minute.
"What?" she croaked. And could have kicked herself for
her confusion.

His interesting smile lines crinkled deeper. "I said there's
no hurry. You're not heavy. What do you weigh...a hundred
pounds soaking wet?"

"Thereabouts," Blair mumbled, caught in the absurdity
of the situation. Where was her composure? The hard-won
confidence with which she now faced the world? "Look."
She sighed. "This is...embarrassing. Just let me down,
okay? Uh, he'll stay there, won't he?" How she hated the
weakness behind her words.

His grin grew wider. "Yes, if I say so. But I swear, he's a
pussycat."

"I'll believe that when I hear him meow!"

Pushing back and letting go, Blair broke loose, dropping
both feet to the ground, keenly aware she'd been able to do
so only because he had let her. Discomfiting thought, that.

But her knee buckled again, tossing her back into the
arms she'd just escaped. So much for standing on her own
two feet!

Two

How's the knee?"

"Tolerable."

"The head?"

"Likewise."

"Good. Hitch yourself a little higher."

Disgruntled, Blair obliged, hiking her body a token inch or so up the broad expanse of his back, feeling the rippling response of hard muscle as he adjusted to her new position. "Okay, Daniel Boone. But I still think this is unnecessary. I can walk—"

"Stow it, dark eyes. And the name's Dom. Dominic Masters."

Wouldn't you know it. Take dominating and add masterful. The name certainly fit! "I'm Blair Mackenzie." Unconsciously, she loosened her grip. "At least let me hold the flashlight."

"With what, your teeth? Now hang on back there. Brutus, let's go."

"We could have stayed—"

"We could not. I have a distinct distaste for foraging bears."

Somehow she couldn't work up a sweat over something she'd barely seen. "He's long gone."

"Not far enough. He considers that huckleberry patch his personal property, and I'm not about to argue."

"I was in more danger from that...that vicious ugly beast of yours." If she had to choose, she was on the side of the bear.

"Ha! Now who's being ridiculous?"

"Who knocked me over?"

"You fell. That 'vicious ugly beast' of mine saved you from a lot worse."

"I hate dogs."

"You'd hate a mad bear more. And you'd better not let Brutus hear you say that."

Blair peeked over the broad plane of his shoulder. The ghastly animal was not only a few feet in front of them on the narrow trail but burdened with two heavy backpacks and therefore no threat. It filled her with a sense of bravado. "What'll he do...bite me?"

"Cry, more likely. He's easily hurt."

"And I'm a ring-tailed monkey."

"Speaking of which, hitch it up another notch. You're beginning to sag."

She hitched. "I'm too heavy for you, Dom. Let me walk."

"Save your breath."

"I'm *trying* to save yours."

"Then don't talk."

I give up! Blair groused to herself, wrapping her arms more securely around his large neck. Dominic Masters was a man with a mind of his own. She hadn't won an argument since she'd come to. Not only that, but being hauled piggyback was undignified, unnecessary, and uncomfortable.

She'd rather hobble, but would the impossible man listen to reason? Ha! He hadn't from the moment he and his fright of a dog had crashed into her life. Within minutes, her gear had been packed, the small fire doused and kicked apart, and she'd found herself sprawled across the broad barn door of his back, jiggling up and down like a yo-yo to the rhythm of his surefooted downhill stride. All *she* knew was they were backtracking the same trail she'd climbed for an unspecified site he said he could find blindfolded.

So how come he'd missed it in the first place? And why wasn't it anywhere on *her* map?

The curious thing was, she trusted him.

Who was this big, purposeful man who, as he'd so casually mentioned, had lugged a chunk of ice miles into the wilderness just to cool a single beer, then didn't think twice about using it on her knee?

Blair was tossing a few more questions around in her mind when a sudden swerve had her skidding across his back like a slick chicken.

"Hey! Signal when you turn," she yelped, clutching fistfuls of wool shirt.

"Sorry. From the gouges in my throat, I thought you had a better grip."

Blair could feel the ripple of his amusement through her own chest as she was unceremoniously hiked back up in place. She had a glimpse of dimly lit foliage in the yellow glow of the flashlight before her eyes sank back to the centerpoint beneath his collar. Something didn't look right. Where was the trail? "Are you sure you know where you're going?"

"That's a hell of a question to ask me now."

"When have I had a chance? If you recall, you just charged in and took over before I could open my mouth."

"Now, now—" he crunched through a thicket as if it weren't there "—I seem to remember a lot of mouth-opening—mostly in the form of leaping meemie screams."

"I happen not to like dogs." Her lofty tone lost effectiveness as she ducked her nose into the shelter of a large shoulder blade to avoid a shower of pine needles.

"So you said. It goes a bit deeper than that, I think. You also haven't told me why."

"Yes, well..." Her scars were her own business. Blair inserted a definite coolness to her voice. "Tell me where we're headed."

"Dead ahead about another hundred yards."

Good. He'd dropped the subject, though she expected it wouldn't stay buried forever. "How can you tell? There's no trail."

"Easy. I just follow my nose."

"Dolt!" She thumped him one on his smug superior back. "Come on, Dom. Are you sure?"

"About as sure as I am of anything in an uncertain world."

"Dominic..." She hoped he could hear the grinding of her teeth.

"Quit worrying, wart. Just hold still back there. All that bouncing around is playing hell on my concentration."

It may have been a teasing remark, but Blair froze, belatedly aware of the potential intimacy of her position. As if she'd bumped into a hot skillet, the heat from his body seared through to her skin everywhere they touched, erasing in her mind the easy relationship she'd thought they had. Warmth changed to a cold prickle of fear. "Put me down! Now!"

Her urgent cry lifted the dark hair around his ear.

"What the hell...!"

He dropped her like a burning briquette. This time she remembered—with the tiny part of her mind that was still functioning on normal—to take the weight on her good leg.

Blair threw her arms around a handy tree trunk and buried her face against the cold rough bark. She must be insane. Going who knew where, for who knew what, with a stranger. The same stranger, mind you, who had that...that *thing* for a pet. No path. No campsite. No humans...and no place to hide.

"Blair..."

The closeness of his deep voice caused a shudder the length of her body, and she tightened her arms around the tree as if it were the last lifeline before she sank. But she wouldn't go down without a fight! If he so much as touched her, she'd bloody his nose! It was so big, she couldn't miss.

"Blair..."

"Go away. Just leave me alone."

There was a moment of silence. "Okay. If that's the way you want it."

Blair's head snapped up. Had she heard correctly?

No. It didn't fit the scenario. "You heard me," she repeated, in case he hadn't. Or she hadn't. "Go away."

"You're sure?"

That spun her around. "Of course I'm sure! I said so, didn't I?" Those damned gray eyes of his, which saw so much and gave away so little, were hidden in deep shadow. The flashlight, half swallowed by his large hand, spread a small pool of light on a thick carpet of the forest's discards—pine needles, twigs, years of accumulated leaves. Her searching gaze reluctantly traveled up, up, and up to smolder on his bold features, which were barely discernible in the dark.

"Well?" she demanded. Just in case, she balled her fists. Just let him try! "What are you waiting for?"

"For you to tell me what's bothering you." Dominic's voice held barely leashed patience. "You came off my back like a scalded cat. What happened?"

"I've had enough, is all! Is that so surprising? You pick me up, toss me around, don't tell me where we're going, scare me half to death—"

"Blair, I—"

"Don't 'Blair' me, Dominic Masters! You may expect blind obedience out of that—that—" Ohmigosh, where was the dog?

Sitting on his haunches not five feet away with his tongue hanging out like a slab of raw beef!

Before she could react, Dom's patience cracked. "Okay, that does it!"

The bellow blasted her back up against the tree. Her shoulders disappeared under his ham-size hands as she was hauled up against the unyielding wall of his body.

Wild-eyed, her face turned a peculiar shade of puce. *"What do you think you're doing?"*

His teeth ground together, filtering nothing from the explosion of his breath. It blew her hair back from her outraged face. "What I should have done hours ago!"

And he kissed her.

Blair's mind went blank. Then adrenaline surged through her system, and she fought free of his arms, dark eyes flashing with indignation. "What was that for?" she demanded.

His voice was wry. "To get your total attention."

"Well, you managed to do *that*, all right," she retorted indignantly. To her inner amazement, the fears of a few moments ago had fled. If anything, she felt a little lightheaded. Delayed reaction from her fall, surely.

"Now that I have it..." In a swift move, Dom swung her off her feet, plunked her on the springy ground, then leaned forward to hunker down on his heels in front of her. "...Let's get a few things straight."

"Such as?" she asked warily, pulse leaping as he placed a big hand on her shoulder.

"A clear understanding of what's going on, for starters." He paused, frowning. "I don't know what caused you to panic, but there's no need for it."

Blair slanted him a speaking look. "I don't know about that."

"Well, you should," Dominic growled, obviously not liking her answer. He took a deep breath, exhaled slowly and looked her square in the eyes. "Look," he said more reasonably, "whether you like it or not, right now you need my help."

Blair's independence took immediate umbrage. "I can take care of myself, thank you."

To her amazement, he flashed her an admiring smile. "From what I've seen so far, and under normal circumstances, I wouldn't be at all surprised. These, however," he reminded her, "are not."

He was right. Beginning to feel extremely ungrateful and not a little foolish for her earlier actions, she held her tongue.

In any event, Dom didn't wait for an answer. "It's late," he said gently. "You're hurt, hungry and tired, all of which I intend to take care of. So quit fighting me every step of the way, Mackenzie." His smile spread to his gray eyes. "All it does is postpone the inevitable."

A typical Masters presumption, Blair decided, finding herself smiling back. "Meaning you won't take no for an answer."

He chuckled. "Look at it this way...a quick camp, a warm fire, and a hot meal served with masterful skill." He shrugged his massive shoulders invitingly. "How can you resist?"

"How indeed." Blair grinned, placing her hand in his as he held it out to her. "Dom, I'm sorry I acted so—"

He cut her off. "Forget it, dark eyes." He stood, pulled her to her feet, held her until she found her balance, then dropped a quick kiss on the end of her nose. "Just think of Brutus and me as a couple of rescuing Saint Bernards."

Her laughter rang out, clear and untroubled, as she raised her eyes to his. "That won't be so hard. You're both so...b-big...." Her words stumbled, then trailed off as awareness came out of nowhere and leaped between them. Her heart pounded and her blood ran hot, then cold, as Dominic's hold tightened on her shoulders.

Half frowning, as if he had no control over his actions, he lowered his head, tilted her chin with his hand and brushed her lips with his.

"Dom..." she whispered.

"Yeah, I know," he murmured in a low growl.

But neither of them moved.

Then he groaned and gathered her hard against his body, and Blair's thoughts scattered as he lowered his mouth to hers.

Soul-destroying, smoldering moments later, Blair surfaced, vaguely aware of his fingers gripping her shoulders, of her heels once more touching the ground. Several things, however, were now very clear in her mind. "Wow!" she said. "Can we try that again?"

His whoop of laughter shook leaves from the trees. Even his dog laughed. Or at least curled his lip, Blair thought with a shred of interest. "Isn't that strange. *Can* dogs smile?"

"Uh-oh. Spatial disorientation."

"Hmm?"

"Never mind." Warmth wove through his deep voice. "We'll talk about it later. You and I, my intriguing dark-eyed hellcat, have one whale of a future, I'm beginning to think. But right now, it's time you were fed and in bed. Move out, Brutus!"

The overburdened dog came to his feet in various stages and lumbered off into the bushes.

Blair was swept back up into massive arms—and large doses of reality—wondering how hot with embarrassment a face could get before it disintegrated.

"Dom, wait a minute." She had to get one thing straight before they went another step—in any direction.

"I knew this was too easy," he said, grinning. "What's the matter now?"

She didn't know any other way to ask, but her mindless response minutes earlier made the question soar in importance. "Can I trust you?" she murmured.

Dominic came to a halt, arms tightening around her small body in recognizable protectiveness. "On my life, Blair."

"That's what I thought. Who are you?" she added, more in wonder than curiosity.

Dominic met her eyes squarely. "I'm a man," he said quietly, "who is attracted to you very much."

"You're not married?" Blair asked, unworriedly, but for good measure. It didn't seem at all strange to be standing in thick woods in the middle of the mountains and asking that. Nor did Dom seem to think otherwise.

"No," he answered softly. "I'm not married. Are you?"

She sighed. "Not anymore." And felt him react as surprise? . . . disappointment? hit him.

His answering rumble was full of purpose. "I'd like to talk about that."

Blair, an intensely private person, didn't so much as hesitate. "Of course."

"You're full of surprises, aren't you, Ms. Mackenzie?"

"Not really."

"I can hardly wait to find out. Meanwhile," he said, brushing past a clump of saplings and into a clearing, "welcome home."

Three

From her vantage point as she sat on her sleeping bag cushioned by a bed of leaves, she was only peripherally aware that the darkness was held at bay by the flames of a crackling fire. Streaks of light and shadow moved over the half circle of meadow sheltered by forest and open only to a swift-flowing stream.

"How is that?" Dominic asked her.

"Mmm."

He shifted the pot in his hand. "And that?"

"*Won*-derful."

"You like it, do you?" He sounded smugly pleased.

Her eyes, narrowed in hedonistic rapture, slanted upward. "You perform miracles," she murmured. "Sure you weren't a sorcerer in another life?"

"Don't sound so surprised. All it takes is a little imagination." His eyes glinted with awareness in the firelight. "Men, after all, have held sway in the field for years."

"Granted, but—"

"But what?" he challenged her with a low growl.

"Oh." Blair looked down at the food in her plate, then widened her eyes, sending him a demure, teasing look. "Perhaps I thought you'd be a little...heavy-handed," she ventured, testing the depth of his sense of humor.

"I may be big, but I hope I'm neither clumsy nor...lacking flair in any endeavor, pint-size." His chuckle was rich with masculine resonance.

Was it also spiced with innuendo? Blair wondered.

"Um," she managed. Having taken quantum leaps forward into intimacy of sorts, she now found prudence in taking one step back. Refocusing her eyes on her plate, she let an easy silence grow.

Dominic Masters, she thought pensively. A massive man. A male of impressive proportions with a deft touch. She took another bite of her Stroganoff, savoring the subtle flavoring he'd introduced into the normally bland trail food. What other surprises might there be in store before he packed up in the morning?

Oh, gosh! The idea of his leaving held diminishing appeal. Now, why was that? she asked herself.

Because, you ninny, you can fool your head and heart, but you can't fool your glands! And *they* ran amok when he kissed you.

What must he be thinking! Blair wondered nervously, avoiding his inscrutable eyes. She'd give a lot to know.

Ho! After her unbidden participation—not to mention enthusiasm!—back in the woods? Surely you jest, Mackenzie, she admonished herself. Chalk up one more knot in the tangle of your life.

But as she forked up the last of her food, Blair didn't regret her decision to take a breather from the gallery. She'd made sure everything was in the works and under control for October's show: the invitation scheduled to be mailed out from the printers, before her return; promises of some "spectacular" mindblowers from her partners and the dependable artisans on her special list.

Something still nagged. Perhaps it stemmed from the rash of unwelcome phone calls from Greg and his mother. She didn't know what the "Deadly Duo" were up to, but they could take a hike!

As she had. Blair smiled to herself wryly, hoping to recharge her energies for the inevitable hassle over the show. Although any job was a snap after working for Greg, sometimes in her role as manager-gofer she felt she was the only glue holding together the artistic temperaments of her six cohorts. Suppose the normal friction—

She jumped as fingers lightly grazed her cheek. Her glance at Dominic confirmed his amusement. "I'm sorry," she blurted out. "Were you talking to me?"

"I thought I was. But you suddenly went blank. I've been trying to make up my mind whether it was the conversation or my culinary efforts that caused it."

"Oh, come on! With the way I've wolfed down my food?"

"Then I'm boring you?"

"That will be the day, my large friend."

"Friend?" His dark brows climbed as his eyes narrowed. "Have we backtracked? If so, I missed it."

Impulsively, she placed her hand on his arm, conscious, so conscious, of the warm strength beneath her fingertips. Maybe she'd get out of this yet. "Could we?" Her voice was soft with entreaty as she searched for understanding in the dangerous territory of his eyes.

"No." His voice was crisp, his mouth set at a purposeful slant in the dark framework of his beard as he rose in a fluid movement. He looked huge and formidable in the flickering light, and very much like a man who never changed his mind.

"Dominic..." Blair had to crane her neck to see his face.

"We'll talk about it in the morning."

"But...aren't you leaving...?"

She caught her breath as he swung on his heel.

"Am I?"

With the fire at his back, she could no longer read his expression. She heard, however, the enigmatic challenge. "Yes, of course," she said with as much conviction as she could muster. "I've taken too much of your time already."

"I'm where I intend to stay, Blair. The decision was made a long time ago."

"Now see here..." she began indignantly, struggling to lay down her plate, get to her feet and mask a strange, forbidding elation. Before she could accomplish anything, a large hand swallowed her shoulder, pinning her in place. The other rescued her plate as it tipped.

"Give me that and stay put. As soon as I get rid of the dinner mess, I'll set up your tent. It's time you were in bed."

Blair gave a swat to his hand. "Never mind that! What about tomorrow?"

His roughened finger against her lips stopped further words cold. His touch sent shock waves to her toes. Trouble. She was in trouble.

The knowledge kept her speechless.

Whether or not he guessed, he flashed her a pirate's grin and strolled off, whistling under his breath, leaving Blair feeling shaken...and exposed.

She'd been sitting with her left leg stretched out, the denim of her jeans rolled up to accommodate the wet compress on her knee. Her right leg had been bent, Indian-style, to form a resting place for her plate. She bit her lip hard, scared to death because his touch was more volatile than anything she'd ever felt, read or dreamed about. Could she find enough strength to fight it?

"Blair."

Her brooding eyes darkened with a flash of anger. While he'd dealt with the pots and pans she'd been dealing with some logical thinking so that by now she had worked herself up into a good, self-righteous mad. Her body might tell her things, but her brain refuted most of it. Not for *her* another relationship. No one would have the power to control her again, present potently sexy company included! Let her belligerence show; she was feeling testy. "What is it?"

"I've arranged a spot for the facilities. Would you like to use it? Do you need my help?"

About to reach for his hand, Blair snatched her fingers back as if she'd been burned. What kind of help? After that kiss—her face flamed in recollection—did he assume she'd be a bonus to his fun-filled weekend in the woods?

Squelching the implosion that thought caused in the hidden regions of her body, Blair squared her shoulders. Appearances to the contrary, she didn't need help from anyone! Answering his questions in order, she snapped, "Yes, I would. And no, I don't."

As if he had his fingertips on her betraying pulse beat, Dom quirked his mouth. "Something's made you grouchy. Indigestion? Or...attraction maybe?"

"I'm not attracted," she said through her teeth.

His grin widened, creating fascinating lines clear up to his eyes. "That may have been true as long as an hour ago. But it's there in your eyes, Blair. And in both our minds." His gaze grew serious, his smile off center, as he added softly, "And it can escalate whenever you give the word."

Obligingly, she gave him a succinct selection of words, which only made him laugh as he hauled her to her feet.

"By the time I get out of this," Blair muttered under her breath as she hobbled toward the trees, "I'm going to have a forked tongue and a knot in my psyche from trying to handle him." Among other things. Which did nothing to lighten her mood.

On her way back, a dark shape loomed, blocking her path. Oh, help! The hairy beast! *Now* what did she do?

Where's your courage? she berated herself. Act indifferent. It can't read your mind! Blair took a cautious step forward.

So did the dog.

She froze in her tracks, cursing under her breath. What were her options? Retreat and get trapped; stand there like a dummy until her knee gave out and pitched her right into his driveling jaws; sneak around his flank . . .

It inched closer. "Dom!" Blair yelled, alternatives forgotten. "Call your dog!"

She stood still as the animal stared back, great tail slashing back and forth, shredding the leaves from the unfortunate bushes.

"Dom!" She knew animals sense when someone is terrified of them. Even she could hear the beginnings of panic. Why didn't Dom answer?

And then he was coming, forging a path through the woods with his large body. "Blair! Where are you?"

"Here," she squeaked, her hand at her throat.

In a few strides he reached her side. All her instincts told her to throw herself into his arms, but her rubbery legs wouldn't work.

"What's wrong?" Even in the darkness she could see the flash of relief in his eyes as he swept her up into his arms. "Are you all right?"

"I'm fine," she managed, hoping she didn't sound as shaken as she felt.

"Hey, come on." His voice softened as he cradled her against his chest. "Did you twist your knee again?"

She felt his heartbeat against the full softness of her breast and a larger fear swept the other away. "No, I'm okay. Put me down."

He did, and she sighed in relief, grateful for the comforting arm he kept around her shoulders. "Actually, it was your dog."

"Brutus? What'd he do?"

"Don't sound so surprised," she answered dryly. "I don't like him, and he doesn't like me."

"Blair," Dom said with exaggerated patience, "what did he do?" He nudged her back toward the campsite with his arm. Using his body and a massive hand, he swept branches aside for her unhindered passage.

"He wouldn't let me past." Blair looked around, couldn't find the culprit and snorted in contempt. The benighted beast had disappeared, too smart to get caught in the act.

"Sunshine, what he was doing was standing guard."

"Over you, maybe. Not me," she denied stubbornly. She'd seen the look in that dog's eye!

Dominic sighed. "Sooner or later you'll realize he's not only a friend but your champion, as well."

"Spare me from both." She shivered with distaste.

His fingers tightened on her shoulder, then he turned her to face him, his eyes searching her face.

Perhaps he could read the pain, the reluctance, the fatigue, she thought. His look changed, and he turned her back toward their camp and her tent, set up so she'd see the sun rise over the tops of the trees.

"We'll talk it all through tomorrow, dark eyes. Right now, get some sleep. Need anything first?"

"No, I—"

"Maybe you don't, but I do," he growled softly. His callused hands cupped her face as he bent low to brush his lips against hers. He lifted his head, eyes sober with emotions she dared not name. "Good night, Blair Mackenzie. I'll...see you in the morning." He added, "Sleep well," and turned abruptly away, calling for the dog.

On an inward wail of warning, she dived into the sanctuary of her two-man tent, lips still blooming from the warmth of his mouth. She shed boots, socks, jeans, shirt and underwear and jabbed her arms and her head into her ankle-length T-shirt-style nightgown. Guarding her knee, she slipped into her sleeping bag and yanked the zipper up to her neck. Staring up at the blue and yellow panels of the thin nylon walls, she listened to the night sounds of Dom settling things down, and she didn't relax until she heard him zip up his sleeping bag.

With a dash of determination she closed her eyes. She would *not* think about him. Instead, you fool, list all the reasons why you'll never be emotionally trapped again, all the other places you could have chosen to hike, the mess on your desk.... Blair's breathing gradually deepened as the day caught up with her.

And as it always did, the dream came from her blind side. She danced around her aunt's big kitchen, pigtails flying, the ruffled skirt of her birthday dress drilling out from her four-year-old legs. The sun was shining, the swing in the backyard beckoning, and the grown-ups too busy catching up to care. How high could she go this year? Wasn't she one year older and a big girl now? She'd surprise them all.

Out the door, down the back steps, her feet skimmed along in shiny new patents, her childish laughter clear in the summer air.

The low snarls made her stumble, and she looked around in sudden fear.

She knew what was coming! Mama, stop it! Don't let it hap—

The black Doberman launched.

Blair woke, hair plastered to her forehead, heart thudding, as her stomach churned in remembrance. Her whole body shuddered and she moaned, fighting off the effects of an incident she hadn't thought of consciously since she was a child. Twenty-eight years old and still threatened by the past. Damn! She shivered again. The trouble with dreams was that they seemed so real. If she hadn't crossed paths with ...

Dominic Masters. Curse him and his dog! Why, of all people, had he and *it* crossed her path? She rubbed fingers up and down her arms to calm the gooseflesh, and nearly jumped out of her skin as her tent flap snapped up.

"Blair? Did I hear you call?" Dominic's deep voice preceded his body as he plowed his head and shoulders into the narrow opening, his large, capable hands reaching out in a determined search for contact. "Are you all right?"

Blair's antipathy evaporated as she was gathered into his arms. For once she welcomed someone else's strength. That there might be pain of another kind to be found there was beyond her ken at the moment. Like it or not, right now she needed rather badly to be held. "I'm okay," she managed. "It was only a dream...."

"A nightmare? My God, woman. You'll never know the scare you gave me in the few seconds it took me to get here." The relief in his voice was an extension of her own now that she was swathed in the security of his warmth. She wrapped her arms more snugly around his rib cage, burying her face in the roughened hair of his torso, loving the strength, the safety, the scent, of being where she was.

His arms tightened. "Those things can be rough, but it's okay now." She heard the soothing words rumble against her ear. "Want me to get you something—?"

"No!" She grabbed him as he started to rise. "No, just let me catch my breath. I'll be all right in a minute."

Her whole body moved with the depth of his sigh. "I'm glad one of us will be." He shifted slightly, deepening the cradle of his arms as he smoothed the damp hair from her temple. "Now," he added almost briskly, "tell me about it."

Her breath leaped. "It was nothing..."

He cut off his low expletive with amazing discipline. "Listen, I've had nightmares aplenty, so I know what it's like. Besides, the only way either of us will get through the rest of the night with any safety at all is for you to start talking."

She'd much rather have heard about him. Pressed hard against his bare chest, Blair weighed the wisdom of opening a personal door. If she did, would he? It was odd, but thinking of Dom's past robbed the demons from her own. She told him.

"Oh, hey." Comprehension deepened his natural earthy rumble. "That explains..." His arms tightened. "You should have told me."

"Well..."

"Never mind. What happened afterward?" His hands moved, kneading the tense muscles around her shoulders.

Blair gulped, aware of heat beginning to build. Keep talking! "Not a whole lot, although it made for strained relations with my uncle for a while."

"I can believe it." Dom's voice—and fingers—flexed. As did the strange sensation in her midsection.

"And...and caused my brother, Jack, a couple of black eyes," she added. *Anything* to defuse the explosiveness of her awareness, to disturb the intimacy rampant in the small nylon enclosure!

"Why was that?"

Thank goodness his hands had stilled. "Oh, you know how it is," she said, attempting to ease herself away. "Taunts when I shied away from anything on four feet. Kid stuff." But hard to rationalize at the time, she thought in retrospect.

"The insensitivity of youth." Far from relaxing, his hold closed, stifling her breath. "I'm glad you had a champion, and I hope he gave as good as he got."

"Better." She smiled. "He was pretty good with his fists."

"I'm glad to hear it. There weren't...other scars, as well, Blair?" Dominic probed gently, obviously wanting to know it all.

One small triangle in the hollow of her left shoulder she'd be insane to mention. "Only to my psyche," she quipped. "Actually, I had a very normal childhood. My family and I spent fantastic weekends nearly every vacation camping somewhere in the mountains.'' Why had she added that? The smart thing to do was close this conversation, remove herself from his unsettling proximity and get him out of her tent.

''Years of experience, therefore unfazed by a little ole bear. Is that it?'' Dominic's tone deepened as his hands began a renewal of slow, insidious destruction to rational thought.

''Something like that. I've...seen them before, certainly.''

''You're a unique woman, Blair. Small, courageous, adventuresome...''

And in a lot of danger! she thought. ''Plenty of others do it.'' Funny how her voice could sound so normal when her mind was following the path of his fingers on her skin.

''But not usually by themselves. Why alone?'' he persisted.

She sensed the narrowing of his interest as she stiffened, gathered herself together and withdrew from his arms as swiftly as she had sought their comfort. ''Personal choice.''

Sending up a prayer of thanks that he made no move to stop her, she turned her back. Her tone cooler now, she said, ''Thank you for your concern. I'm sorry I woke you.'' Polite, dismissing words, she hoped, and made sounds of settling down. ''I'll see you in the morning.''

There was a short, potent silence. Blair held her breath and crossed her fingers. Why didn't he say something?

''Move over,'' he ordered, and she jumped, startled.

''Wh-what?''

''You heard me. You're not sleeping alone.''

''I most certainly am!''

''And *I* most certainly am not going to lie awake all night wondering if you're all right. This way, I won't have any doubts.''

''If this is your idea of a joke...''

"Lady, I'm far removed from any form of laughter. I'm going to get my sleeping bag. If you haven't shifted by the time I get back, we'll be sharing the same side of the tent. Do I make myself clear?"

She had no time to protest. He was up and gone. She wasted thirty seconds in futile frothing and five more scrambling for the tent opening. Did he mean it?

Of course he did! she thought, dismayed. And he was already on his way back, striding on bare feet, sleeping bag slung over one broad shoulder.

Could anything stop him? The only weapon she had was words, which he ignored when they didn't suit him. "This isn't necessary, darn it!"

He came inexorably on, halting only when his big solid thighs were an inch from her nose.

And still she wouldn't back down. There was no way she was going to let him sleep in here. "Dom, there's no need—"

"Don't argue. Move. It's getting cold out here."

So that's why her teeth were chattering—and she could feel her breasts beginning to pucker as the cold seeped through the thin fabric of her gown. "But—"

He ducked low and she reared backward. "Oh, all *right*!" With little dignity, she snaked herself back into what safety there was in her sleeping bag.

He was right on her heels, seeming to overflow the tent's dimensions.

Zipped to her chin, she lay in the darkness, shivering with the confusion of her feelings. The few that were clear made her sink her teeth into her lip.

There was a faint scrape of a belt buckle, the rustle of clothing as he removed his jeans, then the indefinable awareness of padded nylon receiving the sprawled length of a nude, monumentally male body—an image that exploded against Blair's scrunched eyelids.

Imagination, she thought with an ache in her throat, it's a hell of a thing.

It made the silence tick like a time bomb.

"Shall we begin?" he said.

"With . . . with what?" Blair's hands clenched into fists.

Amusement tinged his voice. "How about a bedtime story?"

"Idiot!" Laughter bubbled through her, warming her limbs.

"That's better. Now, get over here."

She was hauled against his body, sleeping bag and all, nestled into accommodating contours and wrapped in the absolute security of arms large enough to keep bears at bay. All before she could formulate a word.

"There. How's the knee?"

"Knee? Oh. *Oh*. Fine." Actually, her attention was elsewhere. His chin rested on top of her head, her hair stirring with every breath he took. Her back—nylon padding be damned—picked out every beautiful nuance of his body curved flush against her spine. And her hips . . . Mackenzie, please! she admonished herself. Don't think about hips.

"Comfortable?"

Sure, she thought disconsolately.

"What's the matter?" he asked, concerned.

Rats! Had she spoken out loud? "Nothing."

He sighed deeply, and she felt the stir of his breath, of his body, from her skull to her knees.

"You question my motives."

"No, no." The denial sprang forth from her lips on a quiver ripe with suspicion. And fear of her own weakness.

"As well you might. But not tonight, dark eyes. Tonight," he growled with regret, "is for holding, for keeping the wolves and the nightmares at bay."

"I don't need—"

"Stow it, Blair. We'll talk in the morning. Now, snuggle down and get some sleep. After the day you've had, you need all you can get."

"All I can get." She sounded like a zombie. What had happened to that cope-with-anything Mackenzie? Normally able to ignore both Greg and his carping mother, she had dropped everything and come searching for a few days of peaceful, uncomplicated breathing space. Which, through circumstances beyond her control, had narrowed frighteningly to the confines of Dominic's massive arms.

Fate. She'd never believed in it, convinced one held one's destiny squarely in one's hands. But now a numbing sense of inevitability seeped into her soul as she listened to his even breathing, felt the rise and fall of his chest against her back, acknowledged the responsive coil of inner awareness that had surfaced back on that trail. His warm, strong embrace seemed to have her pinned hard against the solid mast of a boat embarked on a voyage she had no desire to take.

She knew he wasn't going to leave in the morning. The set line of his jaw had been too easily read, beard or no beard.

Yes, she was attracted to him. Who wouldn't be? He was strong, while Greg was devious; compassionate, while Greg had been too busy to care; virile, while her ex-husband's passion had all been poured into his miserable newspapers.

Oh, blast it! She bit down hard on her thoughts. Don't dwell on the past, Mackenzie, and don't make comparisons. Deal with the immediate.

Which was daunting enough. She buried her nose in her sleeping bag, flexing her resolve. She was strong; she was independent, definitely had herself firmly in control. But she was glad—at least for tonight—that he was here. Perhaps it was the lingering effects of her dream; perhaps not. As Dominic had suggested, "the rest" she would face in the morning.

Her eyes closed as her mind began to drift, and when even in sleep he gathered her closer, Blair's lips softened with a sweet sense of safety. Nothing could get to her through him.

Four

She woke to the *thunk-crack* of splitting wood. A faint whiff of burning cedar teased her nose. Daybreak. Ugh. Much too soon, considering how she felt.

Blair groaned as she turned over, aware of the protest of muscles reacting to yesterday's stresses, the stiff soreness of her knee. Lifting her chin out of the warmth of down-filled covers, she opened one eye for an assessment of her surroundings.

Dominic's sleeping bag was thrown back. She turned her head away, not wanting to think about that at all. She pushed aside the tent flap, propped her chin on both hands and swept her gaze over the perimeter of the campsite.

Mist hovered in a gauzy blanket above the boulder-strewn stream. Against an intense blue background, the first fiery shafts of the rising sun cast golden spears through the tops of the trees on the opposite bank. Closer at hand, the meadow lay christened with tiny pale-blue flowers. Their faint scent mingled in the crisp, pine breeze that stroked her cheek and down the clean line of her throat. A pocket Eden.

And Dominic Masters fit the scene.

His powerful movements as the axe bit into the wood snared her attention. Almost lazily, but with an eye to detail, she traced the play of muscles and tendons straining beneath his well-worn jeans and plaid flannel shirt, which hung loose and open to the waist. He'd rolled the sleeves well up the corded contours of his biceps, and she stared, fascinated with the lines of light and shadow, remembering the feel of those arms as they'd held her during the night.

His hair looked clean, damp, so he must have washed. She swallowed, envisioning him striding nude down to the stream to sluice water over his magnificent body. Primal man in a primitive land.

With a shiver, she flicked the tent flap closed and reached for her backpack. Sparing only moments to fish out clean underwear and a change of shirts, she got dressed, frowning over the bruises surrounding her kneecap. At least the swelling was down.

She was tying the last knot in her hiking boot when the tent flap lifted.

"Hey, you're awake." Dominic's broad shoulders filled the opening as he thrust his dark head forward. His smile matched the devilry in his eyes as he took his time in a perusal of her small person.

"Well?" Her voice was as cool as the morning air.

"Very nice. You might want to add a jacket, though. There's a real nip to the atmosphere around here." If anything, his grin grew wider. "Did you sleep well?"

He knew she had! "Fine, thank you." Blair turned from him as she searched for her down vest.

He cupped her chin, forcing her face around. "How about a proper good-morning, spitfire?"

Her lips parted in protest and fell victim to his mouth. Warm, vibrant, he moved over the surprised contours of her lips with an understated urgency. She lifted her hands in defense, touched, then slid them over the warm ridges of his chest. And she was lost. The cry in the back of her throat matched his aching murmur as she was crushed upward into the heated wall of his body. She put her hands around him, and they seemed to slip under his open shirt with a life of their own; she was swamped with the slick, solid beauty of sinew and muscle rippling beneath her fingertips.

All thought dissolved as his tongue entered her mouth, spiking her inner recesses with stabbing thrusts that had her aching, arching into him in mindless need, feeling his hands curl around her hips. His convulsive thrust against her spawned her cry of agonized want as she damned the barriers keeping them from the fusion she *had* to have.

And then she was free, head back, eyes glazed, mouth still soft and open and moist, still tasting him, dazed with the heady, earthy scent of him...until the bite of his fingers into her upper arms reached her consciousness.

His voice, heavy with remorse, scorched her mind. "Blair, you're...I'm sorry. I didn't intend for that to escalate. Don't move for a minute. I need to get my breath." His ragged tone underscored his words as his arms, gentle now and under rigid command, just held her, giving her time for her blood to cool. Her cheek was pressed against the warm ridge of his pectoral muscles, the male scent of him neither soothing nor soporific.

But when her mind began to function again, she realized how close she'd come to making the worst mistake in her life. She'd made a few so far—Greg being one of them. But she'd recovered. Instinct warned her that this...well, this might well prove to be fatal. That they'd stopped in time, she had only Dominic to thank. A sobering thought.

"Are you okay?"

"Yes, I'm—" she couldn't think of another word "—okay." His murmured concern caused her to stir, separate herself from his embrace.

He let her go, partially. His hands captured her shoulders, and when she dared to look at him, his smile was tender, teasing... and lopsided. "God help us, there wasn't a damned thing *proper* in that at all, was there?" His voice was as shaken as her senses. "You test a man's early-morning resolve."

"Dom, I'm—"

"Shh. It's okay. I know just how you feel. It sneaked up and hit us both between the eyes."

"Dom, you have to know..." She forced the croak from her voice and tilted her chin, eyes as steady as she could make them, as she began again. "You have to know that... that can't happen again."

"Blair—"

"No! Let me finish!" Her nails dug into his arms. "I told you I trust you. *I do!*" she said quickly, overriding his angry protest. "But..." Oh, heaven, this was hard. "I'm sorry I helped let it get out of hand. I don't know what happened." She ignored his "*I* do!" and let conviction fill her eyes as she took another breath. "It was a mistake I won't make again. Please. I'd...like you to leave this morning. It's better for both of us."

Her eyes fell. There, it was said. Well, not all. She wouldn't add that having once been burned, she couldn't afford to play with his kind of fire.

"Blair, I won't let you—"

Hadn't he been listening? she thought, angry now. "What do you mean, you won't *let* me? You might exercise total control over your dog, but you can't control me! *I* make the decisions in my life. Do I make myself clear?"

Dominic's gray-eyed gaze was as grimly intent as hers. "I heard you." His calm voice was edged in steel. "It's also pretty obvious someone in your past tried all that garbage. Now, you listen to me. I have as much desire to control you as I have to slit my throat." His uncompromising hands slid gently down her arms and captured her fingers. He continued to gaze into her eyes as he raised her hands to his lips, brushing purposeful kisses across the silky ridges of her knuckles, entangling her fingers in the curled strands of his beard. When she shivered and tried to pull away, his clasp tightened.

"You are, will always be, your own person," he rasped softly. "But you'll also belong to me. Count on it. Not in ownership but in partnership. As I intend to be *yours* as soon as I can persuade you to take me—make me yours in every sense of the word."

"You're crazy!"

"And determined." He laughed slightly. "I grant you, it may take me a while to convince you, but then—" the full power of his smile made her gasp "—I'm a very persuasive fellow. Or hadn't you noticed?"

"Dominic, you can't—"

"In the meantime—" he lifted roughened fingertips to stroke the halo of mahogany curls at her temples and drop a kiss on the end of her nose "—coffee and breakfast, I think. Then, if you insist, some straight talk and decisions can go full bore ahead. I'm yours to command."

Fat chance she stood, either way! "Dom," she stammered, trying again, "I—"

"Please!" His voice sounded pained. "Not on an empty stomach! I'm totally unreasonable when I'm suffering from unsatisfied hunger."

The devil's own gleam danced in his gray eyes. If her knee didn't ache so hellishly, if her heart would quit slamming against her rib cage and if her tongue would just unglue itself for a minute, she'd throw prudence out the window and flatten his expectations forever more.

As it was, she had no chance. She was all but hauled out of the tent, settled carefully on her feet and, with his muscular arm curved possessively around her shoulder, urged toward a brisk but economical fire that sported a blackened, bubbling coffeepot. In a fulsome frame of mind, she gave no thought to her uneven gait, failing to see his brows gather into a frown.

"You're still favoring that leg. What's the knee look like this morning?"

"Fine," she lied.

"I'll check it after breakfast," he grunted.

"It's *my* knee and it's fine. All it needs are an Ace bandage and a couple of days' rest." She added pointedly, "Which is why I came up here in the first place."

"Is it?"

About to reach for a mug, she glanced suspiciously at his impassive face. Was she reading more into that rather clipped question than was warranted? Either way, more probing would get him nowhere. "Isn't it why everyone comes up here?" she asked, avoiding answering him directly.

"That's very good, by the way."

She raised her head. "The coffee? I haven't—"

"Sidestepping a question with a question." He'd filled his mug, which was almost swallowed by his big hand, but his eyes were on her. And watchful.

With the ease of practice, she filled her own mug from the small pot, limped to a nearby rock and sat, blowing on the hot brew as her fingers cupped around the welcome warmth.

"Yes, isn't it," she finally agreed sweetly. And smiled.

He threw his head back and laughed. From the woods came an answering deep-throated "woof," which jolted her composure, slopped her coffee and almost scalded her fingers.

Darn. She'd all but forgotten that black monstrosity. From the sounds of it, he was mowing down everything in his path to join them for breakfast.

Dominic quickly drained his mug and set it down. "Relax, Blair. He really is harmless."

"Tell that to the woods. It sounds like a massacre in there."

"He's playful."

"He's a one-dog war machine!"

"He's coming— No! Don't move, Blair. He won't hurt you, but if you stand—" he grinned "—or run, he'll think you want to play. I don't expect you'd care to wrestle with a hundred and fifty pounds of puppy."

She froze in the act of rising as the black behemoth came lumbering out of the woods, his great tongue lolling out like the tail of a kite, his back liberally littered with debris from his latest pillage.

"Brutus. Here, boy." Dominic's great arms spread wide as the huge dog hopped and leaped like an eager, ill-arranged bag of bones until he reared, dropping paws the size of an elephant's on Dom's broad shoulders, slopping affection all over his master's face.

Yeck! Blair shuddered again and dropped her eyes to concentrate heavily on her mug. But she raised them almost instantly to watch as the two strong, massive male animals romped all over the meadow in a mad, exuberant game of their own and found herself smiling. Both had unlimited power through sheer size alone, yet each possessed iron control over that amazing strength, using it sparingly, even gently. With some surprise, she heard her own laughter mingle with his and the enthusiastic barking of Brutus as he thudded over on his back, front paws flapping the air in a patently pitiful plea to have his belly stroked.

The expressions on that dog's face were sometimes human, she mused, then shook her head in wry amazement as Dom sat up, clasped his hands around his jean-clad knees and flashed a big foolish grin in her direction.

"Who enjoys that the most, I wonder," she called.

"Guess. Want to join in?"

Immediately sober, she shook her head. With one lithe move, he was on his feet and moving toward her, his smooth, effortless stride, the play of his well-coordinated musculature making her catch her breath. Blair dropped her gaze to her near-empty mug, striving for control of her heartbeat.

"Dark eyes?"

She checked first on the whereabouts of the dog—he was sprawled like a heaving bearskin rug a good twenty feet away—then warily turned her attention back to Dom, not liking at all the purposeful look in his eye. She'd learned to read him fairly well. She stiffened automatically. "Yes, what is it?"

"At least let me introduce him."

"Don't be funny," she said shortly, feeling betrayed.

He held her gaze, which was giving her a crick in her neck, then dropped down, resting on his heels until their eyes were on a level, knees a bare inch from hers. He didn't attempt to touch her, for which she was peripherally grateful. Although it didn't lessen by much the unspoken tension between them.

"Can we talk this out?"

"There's nothing to say."

"Come on, sunshine. Go fifty percent."

"That would be a first. Up to now, I've had to struggle for ten."

"Take advantage of it," he offered, his grin so disarming that some of her belligerence melted. "Okay?"

She'd sound petty if she didn't. "Okay. But it's grudging," Blair warned him for the record.

"Good. That's a start. Now." He rubbed his big hands together in satisfaction. "List all the things you don't like about Brutus."

She looked at him as if he'd just grown horns. "Don't be ridiculous."

"I'm not. Come on. Dig right in. Tear him to shreds. Does he have warts? Sick habits? Bad breath? Is he mean? Too pretty?"

Blair smiled grudgingly. "All right. I get your point."

"I knew you would. Now, is he vicious? Cruel? Threatening?"

"No, but—"

"But he's a dog, right? Now, think of a person you really can't stand."

That was easy. There had been one particular schoolmate she had always hoped God had a hard eye on. "What is this—*Psychology Today*?" she demanded, struggling to rise.

He thrust his hand out, covered her shoulder and refused to move. Which meant she couldn't. Her eyes flashed upward, beginning to narrow with real anger. "Let me up."

"Do you hate all humans because of that one person?" he continued, inflexible persistence uppermost in his voice.

"That's beneath answering. If I'd known you were going to 'grill' me for breakfast, I'd have gone to another restaurant!"

The planes of his bold face dissolved into laugh lines. She heard his rich baritone chuckle as he rose, bringing her along with him. "I can take a hint as well as anyone. It's definitely time for some food."

Hungry enough to call a ceasefire, Blair gave up, allowing him to lead her over to the diminishing fire. Not bothering to hide her irritation, she said, "Why are you pushing so hard, anyway?"

His piratical grin flashed again. "Love me, love my dog. How can I expect to marry you until that's resolved?"

"You can't—on both counts," she stated firmly. "I think you have bats in your belfry."

"And passion in my pa—"

"Hold it right there!"

He smiled with all the innocence of a street urchin. "I was only going to say, 'in my palpitating heart.'"

She stuck her fists on her hips. "Change the subject, Mr. Masters."

"Sourdough pancakes?"

"Better. There's hope for you yet. Did you really haul along some batter?" After the beer and ice, why was she surprised? The man did exactly as he chose.

"Never travel without it. Nor a special carton of honey the likes of which you won't believe." He gave her a quick hug, fed bits of wood to the fire and came back to refill her mug.

"I thought all *seasoned* backpackers measured their gear in ounces." She held her breath as he lifted her chin, his fingers hard and sure against her skin.

"Some things are worth the extra effort. Remember that."

"Are we still talking about food?" She bit her lip defensively, ignoring the invitation in his voice and the sudden dip in her stomach. Blast him! His expression could be bottled and sold as "sin."

"For the moment. Now, sit still and watch a master at work."

She already had—if that episode in the tent was anything to go by. Blair shivered in the escalating warmth of a strengthening sun. What was she going to *do* with this man?

One erotic suggestion shot into her mind in exquisite detail, and she blushed straight to her toes.

Five

It wasn't fair, Blair thought as she watched Dom making them a gargantuan breakfast. After calm years of slumbering, her libido had chosen a fine time to resurface. *And* over a mammoth stranger she knew nothing about, which said volumes for the state of her mind.

"Dominic, who are you?" Her question had broken a long silence, and he raised his head. She caught the flash of humor in his clear eyes before he lowered them again to concentrate on the bubbling griddle.

"Now, that's an odd question. I thought I'd answered that back in the tent."

His tone nettled her. "Oh, come on. You know what I mean."

"Hold your fire. I didn't mean that flippantly. Give me a minute here." Dom finished lopping pancakes onto tin plates, slavered the steaming stacks with butter and honey, then brought them over to where she sat and dropped down beside her. "I'm prepared to bare my life and my soul anytime you are."

"You have a strange way of showing it. Every time the subject comes up, it seems to get changed." Blair settled her bottom more firmly on her rock and accepted the smaller helping with alacrity.

"Not intentionally, I assure you. But for both our sakes, do you suppose we could suspend conversation until after breakfast?" he asked politely. "I don't know about you, but I'm fading fast."

As she was, come to think of it. If food was delayed much longer, her stomach would post picket lines and go out on strike. What could she do but grin and agree? "All right, I suppose so. It looks wonderful."

"Wait'll you taste 'em. Dig in while they're hot."

She did, and her eyes widened in amazement. "They *are* good!"

"Of course." He managed to look offended as he dug into his own plate. "Would I lie?"

"How do *I* know?" she sighed, hoping her shrug held adequate drama. "The only thing I have to go by is what you tell me. But I remember what Grandma always said...." She paused delicately.

He chuckled around his next mouthful. "Okay, I'll bite."

She ignored the pun—if one had been intended. "'Never trust a man with a gleam in his eye, glib on his tongue, or grizzle covering his chin,'" she quoted. "'Nine out of ten, girlie, he's got something to hide.'"

He grinned wolfishly, reaching out a long arm to replenish their coffee. "Was she speaking from experience, do you suppose?"

Blair laughed. "Knowing her, she could have been, but both she and my dad were very circumspect. Grandpa even more so. I never heard so much as a rumor."

"Umm. An inherited trait, I believe."

Instantly wary, Blair focused her gaze on the last of her breakfast. "I don't know what you mean."

"Garbage. You're doing it now. The minute I say anything remotely serious, you close up on me. You know I'm as interested in who you are as you are in me." Dom's voice lowered somewhat in volume. "From what little you've said so far and a lot you haven't, it's obvious you've been deeply hurt. Your marriage ended. Was it through death or divorce?"

Startled into honesty, she answered. "Divorce."

"Okay." He exhaled heavily. "Then I hope you'll trust me enough to eventually share the whys and hows of it. But one thing you can count on without reservation. You're safe with me." He smiled with aching tenderness. "You're stuck with me, and I will never hurt you in any way."

"That's nice to know," Blair managed, not sure which she was referring to.

"Yes, it is," Dominic stated firmly. "We've all been hurt at one time or another. But the past has no place in the future. This is the here and now. And you know how it is with us, Blair. One touch and we both go up in flames. It's hit me deep in my gut, yet I'm doing my best to show restraint, giving you time to get used to it."

He leaned forward, and she stopped breathing as he continued, his voice low, deep, implacable. "I can't explain it any more than you can. I don't even want to try. Neither am I going to let this—or you—slip from my fingers. I know we were destined to more than meet, regardless of what you may think, no matter how hard you fight it. As for the vital statistics—" he grinned, ignoring the slightly stunned expression on her face "—I'm thirty-four, financially solid and remarkably kind to both man and beast. I'm also the apple of my widowed mother's eye. And now, my dear Blair, it's your turn."

The verbal onslaught had caught her with her fork halfway to her mouth, which hung open. Blair dropped the former and closed the latter, wishing to heaven she'd never started this conversation. She had forgotten that sharing was a two-way street. And from the relentless look in Dominic's eyes, he was going to sit here until she reciprocated. Touched by his words far more than was perhaps wise, she nevertheless strove for an offhand answer.

"Okay," she said finally. "I'm twenty-eight, financially holding my own, also kind to man, but not so tolerant of beasts." His devious dog headed the top of her list.

If Dom was disappointed in her answer, he kept it hidden. "I'm a man," he said softly. "Does that kindness extend to me?"

"That's what I'm afraid of," she answered without thinking.

"Don't be," he said swiftly. "Not of me nor of your feelings."

She hadn't meant to make him frown. Or offer any encouragement. "I'll give it some thought," Blair commented lightly, turning her attention back to her plate. How could she have answered him truthfully when, sexual attraction aside, she couldn't sort out her real feelings? This—whatever "this" was—was happening too fast. For Pete's sake, instead of probing for information right off the bat this morning, why hadn't she said something nifty like . . . like . . . "Are there any fish in that stream?"

She'd meant merely to change the subject, not get a reaction that made her blink.

"Damnation!" Dominic lunged to his feet. "I hope it's not too late! Are you through?"

Before she could answer, he'd swiped plates, forks, mugs and coffeepot out from under her nose and deposited them in one big heap near the fire. "Don't touch these," he commanded her. "I'll get them later."

Two long strides and he was hunched over his enormous pack, muttering and mucking about in its innards until he gave a pleased growl and came back looking like a satisfied clam. "You, Ms. Mackenzie, God willin' and the creek don't rise, are invited out to dinner."

"Oh?" As she was yet unable to see what had caused all the excitement, Blair's curiosity rose. They were miles from civilization...as if that could possibly stop him. "Am I permitted to ask where?"

"Sure." His grin grew. "A private little riverside café. Right over there by that posh pile of rocks. Nothing formal, you understand, but veddy, veddy exclusive."

"Why, how nice," she drawled, amused. "I'll be sure to do my nails." Blair had finally identified the fishing rod he was swiftly assembling. For someone so huge, he had a smooth quickness with a fluid mastery. She liked to watch him in motion, follow the ripple of muscle along his generous haunches....

Aware of a silence, she raised her eyes. Dominic's gaze held a look that hit her in the solar plexus, and she quickly glanced away, willing her face not to change color.

"Would you mind very much if I left you alone for a couple of hours?" he asked after a moment. "The sun's almost too high, but I'd promised myself something special for our dinner, and there's this deep pool..."

"Uh-huh. With the granddaddy of all trout," she finished for him.

Dominic chuckled. "Not quite so stereotyped. But I've had good luck often enough to be able to promise enough for a meal."

"You've fished there before?"

"Yes, often."

"So that's how you found this place in the dark. And why you hadn't planned on leaving this morning. You might've told me."

"You hardly gave me a chance."

She conceded him that. "How often do you come up here?" Blair did a little fishing of her own.

"Oh, two or three times a year," Dom answered absently, preoccupied with line and reel. "These scrappy little devils are worth coming up for—although, to tell you the truth, I'm a saltwater man at heart."

"Which means, I suppose, that you own a boat?"

"Doesn't everyone in and around Seattle?" He grinned.

"There are a few of us who've refrained," Blair answered dryly. "What kind is it?"

"A cabin cruiser that can take anything Puget Sound dishes out." It sounded like a challenge he relished.

It made Blair shudder.

"I hope you're into boating." Seemingly satisfied with the results of his efforts, Dom turned his attention back to her.

"Sorry. It's not my cup of tea. I get seasick looking at all that water, even on a calm day."

"We'll have to work on that, sunshine." His grin made her knees weak. "Meanwhile, time's a-wastin' if I expect to wine you and dine you as promised." His voice softened as he rose. "I'd much rather have you with me, Blair, but you'd better stay off that lovely limb of yours. Besides, there're a couple of bad spots I have to beat my way around. Sure you'll be all right alone for a while?"

"I'm perfectly fine on my own." Now, and in the future. She'd have to remind herself of that on a regular basis until she was out of this wild situation and back in the security of a world she understood.

He leaned forward suddenly, catching her unaware, to brush her lips with his. "Do me a favor," he murmured against her mouth.

What? Her lips said the word silently as she tasted honey, and coffee, and intoxicating male in a dizzying kaleidoscope of impressions.

"Miss me a little." It was more command than request as he withdrew slightly, holding her gaze as her heart turned over. She could easily drown in the gray depths of those eyes.

Blair backed mentally away. Everything warned her to keep it light. "Fat chance, braggart. Go catch yourself a fish . . . if you can."

"Challenges. I love them." He laughed, running a seductively gentle finger along her jawline. "I ought to warn you, though. I usually win."

No doubt. Confidence surrounded him like a second skin, the bronze of which looked good enough to . . . Darn! Blair pulled a halt to her thoughts. "We'll see, won't we?" she answered with a challenge of her own, hoping his hearing wasn't acute enough to pick up the jackhammer of her pulse.

"That's a promise I'll remind you to keep, Ms. Mackenzie. Be warned."

She was. If she could get her head to listen.

As he pulled on a down-filled vest and extracted a disreputable-looking cotton hat from its pocket, Blair watched in silence, amused by the collection of brilliantly hued fishing flies that were attached over most of its surface. It seemed he threw himself heart and soul into every endeavor, a point she'd do well to remember.

"Which reminds me," Dom added, giving her a stern look. "Stay off that knee. Take a nap while I'm gone. And don't be fooled by that stream. It may look harmless, but it's deep in spots, and the current is a lot stronger than you might think."

There were a lot of things she could say—*should* say—but she bit back her indignation. Time enough later to rock him back on his size-twelve heels. "I'm not exactly a novice at this, remember?"

Her tone might have been tempered, but she couldn't disguise the flash in her eyes.

Dominic's acknowledging grin reached to his brows. "But you're cute," he teased, "no bigger than a minute, and mean very much to me. So take care. That's all I'm saying."

Before she could take issue, he had jammed the hat on his great head and was striding off, whistling Brutus to his side. Good heavens. She'd actually forgotten the big brute.

Which once again made her question her state of mind.

Reluctantly, Blair turned to watch the two impressive figures disappear behind a screen of underbrush near the stream's low graveled bank. In the loud empty silence, she took a deep breath, then let her shoulders slump, feeling unaccountably left out, foolishly lonely and not a little afraid because of it.

What had happened to her anger? Blair wondered and looked around the quiet campsite as if she'd find it hanging somewhere in the early-morning air.

For that matter, what had happened to her thinking? *And* to the confident control she thought she had over her own destiny? How could one man—*that* man—leap into her life and shake its foundations so quickly?

Teasing her out of a temper, wooing her with words, melting her socks in her shoes with his kisses . . .

Oh, help! Blair forced some indignation into her system as she ran an agitated hand through her hair.

Come to think of it, wasn't there something insulting about "cute"?

And orders. Stay off the knee. Take a nap. Love me, love my dog. A take-it-for-granted-she'd-do-it echo of the past when she'd been expected to eat, breathe, sleep and snap to when told. All at someone else's whim, never hers. She certainly couldn't envision Dominic submitting to orders. Just the thought made her snort inelegantly.

Well, neither did she. Personally, she'd had them up to her ears, a fact Bea and Greg had had a hard time learning to swallow.

Blair frowned. Which might explain the change in their recent tactics. Her mother-in-law, in fact, had sounded almost pleasant, while butter would have surely melted in Greg's mouth.

Familiarity bred not only contempt but suspicion, as far as she was concerned. It was obvious to her they each wanted something. What it could be, time, prodded by their impatient natures, would tell. Well, she could handle them, so she could certainly handle Dominic.

The oh-so-confident Mr. Masters might believe the past had no place in the future, but experience had taught her otherwise. If smart, one learned from one's mistakes. And knuckling under rated first place on her list of "never mores," Blair thought grimly.

Compliance. The old peace-at-any-price syndrome. It had gained her nothing but cost her dearly. As had sexual attraction, she admitted with customary candor, coming to her feet and remembering Greg's tall blond blue-eyed intensity when they'd first met.

And just look where that had landed her. Married to an ambition-ridden husband, forced to live with a reluctant, opinionated mother-in-law, then coerced into postponing her own career to support Greg in his. Goals were something she understood; mania—Greg's thirst for success—had been something else.

And no one had ever prepared her for Bea. She'd never met anyone before or since, thank heaven, who could combine a two-pronged tongue and a demand for either obedience or attention with such deadly skill. By the end of a sad, disillusioning year, she had realized her self-respect lay somewhere around her ankles and that her marriage was over.

From there it had been a slow climb, both mentally and psychologically, to where she now stood.

Which just happened to be smack in the middle of a vast untamed wilderness. Blair smiled as an influx of natural humor brought her attention back to her surroundings. Sharing a small paradise with one of the most demanding, disarmingly dangerous men she'd ever had the fortune—or *mis*fortune—to meet had to be on a par with thumbing one's nose at the gods. It was all right if one was prepared to take the consequences. She, she decided, was not.

Blair's gaze flickered to the tent. It looked harmless, a vibrant splash of color against the dark background of the deep primitive forest. But her heart, mind and body quivered with the memory of a shared mutual explosion of passion within its intimate confines. *Mutual* passion.

Her knees gave way and she dropped back down on the rock. A few moments out of time. That's all it had been.

Yet despite all her defenses, the sensual song still sang through her bloodstream, and her thoughts were anything but sane. What would it be like to feel him deep in her body?

Oh, no! Blair leaped to her feet and staggered down to the stream, needing cold water on her face, on her limbs, to conquer the heat scorching her thoughts.

What was she going to do with this man? And hadn't she asked that before? She'd better come up with an answer before he got back!

Using her shirttail to dry her tingling face, Blair limped back, circled the dying fire and, settling on her rock, pulled some resolution up from her bootstraps. She frowned. It ought to be easy to think her way out of this dilemma, she thought, considering her past subjugation, a long string of broken promises, the trials of living with the selfish son of a vituperative mother. It still left a bitter taste in her mouth.

She stared down at her hands. To be truthful, it was coffee, a faint hint of honey and the lingering male essence of Dominic that now lay on her tongue.

Sighing, Blair came to her feet, shaking off both sets of disturbing memories. She would do well to remember who she was, she thought with a belligerent shake of her shoulders. An independent woman immersed in an artistic career she adored, with neither time nor inclination for romance, sex, an emotional relationship... or the masterful magic of Dominic Masters.

As for his high-handed orders. Well, a wealth of experience had taught her a lot. Including how to say no. A simple but effective word, no. "Either way, you have a fight on your hands, you devastating devil," she warned, and got to her feet. "Blair Mackenzie does as she damned well pleases these days."

Her heart picked up a beat as her eyes lit with decision. A small but deliberate show of independence now might save her a lot of trouble later on. Taking a deep, satisfying breath of the pure mountain air, she let a bubble of anticipation take the form of an uninhibited grin. Defying Dom held pure elements of excitement.

Didn't it just.

Blair laughed outright and rolled up her sleeves.

Six

———

Humming with energy, and against Dominic's specific instructions, Blair limped through the campsite, cleaning away their breakfast mess. She then stowed their separate gear into neat patterns of her own choosing until her artistic eye was satisfied.

She chopped kindling enough to see them through tomorrow's breakfast, when, she assumed, he'd have to strike out for civilization if he had come up just for the weekend.

In the middle of stacking her final load, Blair paused, unable to sort relief from regret at the thought of his leaving at *any* time. Where would their brief relationship have taken them by then?

"*You* make the choices, Mackenzie. Remember that!" Blair blew straggles of damp mahogany curls away from her overheated forehead as she dumped the last of the wood. "It will go as far as *you* want it to and not another step further."

She stood, hot, thirsty and tired in the heat of the mid-morning sun, remembering the feel of his hands on her body, the vital warmth of his mouth, and shivered. Was it any wonder she was worried?

"Don't think about it!"

Good advice she was going to heed the rest of the morning. Grabbing a pot, she limped down to the stream for cold, fresh water, then dumped in a packet of dried lemonade with a vigorous stir. Leaving it to settle on a handy tree stump, Blair then turned toward her tent. Working on a tan had been part of her original plans. She refused to call it a rest, even if Dominic was right about her knee giving her fits.

By now the air inside the nylon enclosure was stifling, so Blair made quick work of stripping out of her heavier clothes and into a stretchy peach tube top with matching shorts. Then, armed with sunglasses, beach towel, tanning lotion, and a fat paperback with a cover lurid enough to inflame even an aesthete's imagination, she backed out of the tent and poured herself a full mug of lemonade. She was going to do this in *style*.

Looking militant and feeling more like a lame, overloaded duck, Blair padded on bare feet to a sunny spot in the meadow, spread out her accouterments and sank to the ground with a satisfied smile. This was more like it, she thought, smoothing a thick layer of protective cream over her skin, frowning when she came to her knee. Even through her sunglasses she could detect the varying shades of discoloration. At least the region felt less tender under her fingertips than it had yesterday.

Dismissing it from her mind, she let her gaze and her spirits drink in the summery silence of her surroundings as she turned her face up to the sun.

The only sounds she could hear were the drowsy drone of insects and the muted pleasurable rushing of the nearby stream; the only decision she had to make was which side to tan first—front or back. A definite change from her normal routine.

Blair smiled as she opted for back first and buried her nose in the warmth of her beach towel. If she could toast herself like this for a week, she'd be tanned, rested and teeming not only with energy but perhaps some fresh approaches to implement all over the gallery. Although the theme—Spacial Dimensions—was set for their big fall show, she intended to add her personal touches here and there for contrast, color or special focus.

She felt her smile and her heart grow as warm as the sun on her back as her thoughts drifted homeward. Living in the oddly shaped apartment above the gallery kept her square in the center of a career she adored. To some her life might appear insular. They didn't know her partners! A more complex, eclectic, outgoing group would be hard to find. In the beehive activity of a working gallery, her life with them was day-to-day discovery.

It was rare to find seven artisans in action under one roof, which was certainly one reason for their success. Whether wielding a propane torch, working away at a loom, or refinishing a prized antique twenty feet from a jeweler forging silver sheet into beautiful textured shapes, she and her partners offered customers the same sense of discovery, of kinship, and an important voice in the design of their purchases.

Blair stretched like a contented cat, turned over onto her back and pushed her sunglasses up on her nose, feeling pleased and vindicated by the past six years of hard work.

It definitely had had other rewards as well, she admitted with a rush of gratitude. Renewed self-worth, total independence, a select group of well-tested friends and professional acquaintances—Maggie Cappelini, for one—whom she could trust implicitly.

Blair's eyes crinkled as she envisioned the older woman, who had been so instrumental in finding the adequately zoned building Blair now called home. In her late sixties or early seventies, yet still a high-powered dynamo realtor, Maggie knew not only most everyone in the city but anyone *worth* knowing in the art world, and she'd been like a professional Snow White to seven slightly oddball, anxious dwarfs at the time. It hadn't occurred to her until now, but for all of her friend's openness, Blair really knew little of Maggie's personal life, other than that she had a son, Doc, who lived with her. Unmarried—and no wonder, Blair thought. From what she'd gathered, he was devoted to his work, rarely home and set in his ways when he was.

Having been involved with an iron-willed, self-centered workaholic herself, Blair could sympathize with her. Then she smiled, wondering how Maggie would react if she ever met Dominic.

Ha! She'd fall over her well-shod feet like any other woman worth her salt. Blair groaned, giving up trying to keep the impossible man out of her mind for more than five minutes at a time.

Would he catch his limit and be back soon? Would her stomach stop leaping around like a thing possessed when she thought of the hours ahead? Of the night she had to somehow get safely through in his company?

And out of his arms?

Blair's eyes snapped open as her heart sagged clear to the back of her spine. Great. Simply great. She'd just managed to spoil a perfectly peaceful morning.

It wasn't the heat of the sun making her palms sweat and her hair stand on end. Grimacing, she sat up, sipped some of the now-warm lemonade, then resolutely lay back down.

Clear your mind. Take deep breaths. *Uncurl your toes, Mackenzie!*

Think soporific. Serene. See? It was simple.

It lasted less than a minute.

An agonized howl brought her bolt upright, wondering who on earth was being strangled. The mournful moan sounded again. It seemed to come from the stream, but with the sun's dazzling reflection off the water, she couldn't locate a thing.

More curious than alarmed, Blair came to her feet and walked, tenderfooted, toward the gravel bank. A series of sharp barks zeroed her eyes on the source, and Blair made a sound of disgust. What she'd thought at first was a soaked pile of debris draped over a boulder was a dark bedraggled pile of *dog* draped over a boulder. Not satisfied with rampaging through the woods, Brutus was now terrorizing the fish.

Blair immediately lost interest. If he was howling because he was stuck, it was just too bad. He'd gotten himself there; he could get himself back.

She turned away, and the dog went into a frenzy, barking and howling and shaking his furry mane as if to freeze her in her tracks. He almost succeeded.

"I'm not afraid of you, you flea-bitten lummox," she yelled crossly. Which was true with the distance between them.

And then she saw the blood. To her horrified eyes, it seemed to be pumping out of his left front leg in spurts, changing the water to an ugly red froth. It made her slightly sick.

It also made her angry. *Who had done this to him?* And what did he expect *her* to do? Dammit, where was Dom? It was his dog, his responsibility. She looked around the meadow, and the emptiness twisted her insides. It was up to her; she'd known it all along. And so had the dog.

"You benighted beast," she said, seething. "I'll bet you did it on purpose!" Too furious to remember her fear, Blair surged into the water, flinching at both the cold and the strength of the current. She promptly stepped in a hole, went under and came up sputtering and swearing as she finally got close enough to lunge for the dog.

"Come on, boy. Here, Brutus. Let's go." Blair made a grab for the rock, fighting the current, fearing the cold seeping into her legs.

"Come on! We've got to get you out of here!" Blair tugged at the deadweight, frustrated and feeling helpless. She was getting nowhere fast.

"Listen, you ungrateful mutt!" she cried. "Get off that rock!"

The animal dropped his head and closed his eyes.

"You die on me and I'll kill you!" Blair yelled. Oh, God. What order had Dom given yesterday when—?

She had it! Now she prayed that it worked. She took a deep breath and lowered her voice to a growl. "Brutus! Protect!" she commanded, and threw herself to one side.

The big dog lurched like a cannonball, coming down so hard in the water the backwash dragged her under. Blair did a complete flip and broke to the surface, surprised it was only waist deep. The ingrate, she saw, had finally gotten the idea, and was plowing to shore, so Blair floundered along in his wake, on the one hand wishing she were close enough to *boot* him the rest of the way, on the other wishing her first aid weren't so rusty.

Not bothering to stop once she reached shore, she staggered past the dog's prostrate form, grabbed an extra towel and limped back, teeth sunk into her lower lip, knowing what she had to do. She took a deep breath, then dropped to his side.

As best she could, Blair ignored the pain in his eyes as she gently patted the wound dry so she could assess the damage. Oh, gosh! It was going to need stitches. She wasn't prepared for this, having neither the skill nor the right equipment. But if she tore up a shirt—

At the thud of footsteps she lifted her head and slumped in relief as Dominic came on a dead run, his face rigid and intent, mouth as grim as his eyes as they swept over the scene, not missing a detail, she was sure. He dropped his gear and in three steps was by her side, his hands swallowing her small shoulders, eyes questioning and dark with emotion. "Are you all right?"

"Yes," she assured him hurriedly. "But Brutus is hurt."

"What happened?"

As she told him, Dom's dark brows raised and his fingers dug into her shoulder blades. She hardly noticed. To her they felt urgent, warm and exceedingly welcome. "He's going to need stitches," she added, coming to the end.

"I'll take care of it in a minute. Let's get you warm and dry. Your skin is like ice."

"I'm fine," Blair said impatiently. "The dog isn't."

Dominic's face tightened. "You first, Blair. Always. Come on."

As he lifted her to her feet, she slapped his arms away. "Listen, I didn't rescue that mangy mutt to have him bleed to death! If you won't do it, I will!"

Dom's smile was patient and inflexible. "I assure you, I'll look at him, but you need to get warm, pronto. Hypothermia—"

"I'll get a shirt," she snapped.

"Better yet," he said, suiting words to action, "take mine. It's quicker." He took off his flannel shirt and draped it over her shoulders. "This should help temporarily. Peace?"

Blair gave in. It was, after all, an acceptable compromise. "Peace," she agreed with a sigh as she hugged the shirt's—and his—welcome warmth to her body. Warmth, she suddenly realized, that actually reached past her knees. She felt as if she'd been swathed in a mammoth-sized blanket. Great heaven but he was a huge man. For some reason that thought sent a shivery sensation up her spine. "Where do you get your clothes," she quipped as he knelt to examine the dog, "Omar, the tent maker?"

He laughed. "Are you sure you're okay?"

"I'm fine. How about him?" she asked, feeling her answering smile fade.

"You were right," he said after a moment. "It has to be sewed." Dominic glanced up at her. "Keep the towel in place while I get my kit. I'll be right back." With the effortless speed she was beginning to recognize, he was gone and back.

Blair moved out of his way and watched with growing interest as Dom opened a surprisingly well-equipped bag.

"This shouldn't take long." His motions were calm and steady, his voice quiet as he spoke to the dog. His touch seemed sure, gentle, skilled.

"Is there anything I can do?" Blair thought to ask. "I've had a little experience."

Dominic glanced up, interested. "You have? Where?"

"I worked as a girl Friday for an eye, ear, nose and throat specialist during my first year in college."

"How about that. Any in-house surgical procedures?"

"A few," Blair answered, watching him cut away the fur around the wound. It looked as if he knew what he was doing, at any rate. "Tonsillectomies, that sort of thing," she elaborated. "Although he removed a carbuncle from the foot of a friend one time." She dimpled at the memory. "After hours and strictly on the qt."

"I'll bet," Dominic answered dryly. "Look, can you try to keep his leg still? I'm going to sew this up, and in spite of a topical anesthetic, it's going to pinch."

Blair gulped, glancing apprehensively at the woeful expression on Brutus's face. She couldn't stand to see anything suffer. "Sure," she answered, and vowed to close her eyes.

But by the time it was over, Blair's dark eyes were wide-open and speculative, as were her thoughts. While she had changed into dry clothes, Dom had bound Brutus's leg, rekindled the fire and was ready to hand her a mug of fresh coffee as she emerged from the tent.

She followed him over to perch on her rock as he lowered himself to the ground beside it. They sipped in silence for a moment, then Blair glanced toward him, her eyes faintly accusing as they met his. "You knew I'd notice your skill. You're a doctor. A . . . a surgeon."

Although Dominic's face looked composed, there was a decidedly wicked gleam in his eyes she found hard to interpret.

"Only in a manner of speaking," he replied.

"Oh? What's that supposed to mean?" Blair asked suspiciously, then took a sip from her mug.

"That I operate . . . but out of a cat house."

The coffee caught in her throat and tried to come out her ears.

Seven

That was warped even for a specializing vet!'' Blair eventually managed to gasp. Her dark eyes *dared* him to explain or to thump her on the back one more time.

"Sunshine. I said I was sorry. It's an old in-house joke."

"Save it for your claw-footed clients." She sniffed, holding on to her indignation with slippery fingers. Dominic's mouth was under control, she noted, but his eyes still danced with laughter. "You're not the least bit repentant, you wretch."

"I couldn't resist," he admitted with no shame at all.

"I noticed." At her dry tone he brought his gaze to hers. Blair fought to suppress a grin. It *was* pretty funny in retrospect, but she'd never give him that satisfaction. He was too confident as it was.

"That's my girl. Did you miss me this morning?"

Too much for safety. "Did you catch anything?" she countered.

"Ah, a very good question. There's definitely something fishy planned for later." He grinned with an open leer. "Don't tell me you had any doubts."

Plenty! But they had nothing to do with his skill as an angler. "I'll bet what you have in mind and what *I* have in mind aren't quite the same thing."

"Oh, I don't know. I imagine our thoughts are more similar than you think."

"Careful there, Mr. Masters. When it comes to fresh-caught trout, I don't fool around."

Thank heaven he *couldn't* read her mind. He was sitting far too close for comfort, invading the precious perimeters of her personal space and making a mockery of all the resolutions she'd raised earlier when she'd been alone and able to think straight.

His misbegotten dog was no help either, she thought miserably, eyeing that thick-furred, snoring, oblivious heap. For once, she would really welcome the intrusion. Anything to break her awareness of Dominic's body.

The meadow simmered with heat. So did he. So did she. His strong teeth flashed white against the rich dark wealth of his beard, his eyes—so gray and clear and frankly beautiful as he looked at her—made her heart turn over. She watched as he raked a huge hand through his unruly hair, then froze as he leaned even closer, looking overpoweringly virile and magnificently male.

Before she could think to move, with a strangely intimate gesture he stroked that hand over her damp curls and down the sudden heat of her neck, letting his fingers stretch over her shoulder to come to rest on her collarbone. His touch was an inch away from her pulse, she thought in panic as he bent his head, his breath a warm, fragrant caress against her cheek. He looked good enough to eat.

"Are you hungry?"

"Yes," she blurted, too late to stop the word.

"Then I guess I'd better feed you." He got to his feet reluctantly, and Blair shivered at her near escape.

Dom's quick eyes caught the goose bumps on her arms. He dropped back down on his heels and ran his hands over her telltale skin. "Are you sure you're not cold?"

Was he kidding? She could fry an egg on her forehead. "I'm fine," she managed.

"You looked so beautiful," he rumbled softly.

Oh, help. So did he. "Thank you," she answered, despairingly aware of tangled hair and her scrubbed-clean face.

"You remind me of a dark-eyed, curly-topped chrysanthemum, all silky petals and vibrant with color."

Make that a stir-fry, Blair thought bleakly as her facial heat increased, stilling her tongue.

"By the way, do you like cats and soft, furry kittens?" he murmured.

It raised images of being stroked in her mind. Oh, Dominic. Don't *do* this! "They make me sneeze," she said, then gulped. Mentally she might be leaning away, but her shoulders homed in on the hollows of his hands as if they were made to fit.

"Holy smoke. Are you telling me you're allergic to cats?"

"I don't know if I am or not." She wished he'd button his shirt. The bronzed girth of his bare chest seemed to draw her eyes like a magnet, raising tactile memories that made her heart pound and her throat go dry. She dragged her eyes away and made her mouth move. "But I sneeze whenever they're around."

"Mmm." Dominic looked thoughtful for a moment, then his brow cleared. "Okay, that should be no problem. Brutus always mothers them out of their minds, so I don't keep any at home."

"Problem?"

"With you kerchooing all over my bed."

That snapped her eyes around. "I'm not—"

"*Yes* you are. Or will eventually." He grinned. "Just give me time."

"That's not all I'll give you, you arrogant baboon!" Blair wrapped the words in good-natured banter, determined to treat the situation like a joke while she still could. "Didn't someone mention lunch?"

"Hoist by my own petard." Dominic sighed as he surged to his feet. "I'm going to have to work on my timing. Okay, you hungry hunk of delectability, what'll it be? Gorp, granola bars, crackers with some kind of cheese squeeze, dried soup, dried fruit, Vienna sausages, s'mores..." His eyes lit. "That's an idea. Want s'more, Blair?"

"Dolt!" Her laughter joined his as she stood. "What, may I ask, happened to the big catch of the day?"

"You're lookin' at him." His eyebrows waggled as he threw his arms wide. "Wanna reel me in?"

"Nope. Too easy. Now, if I were a fisherman, I'd like a little more resistance from my fish. Besides, I thought..." She'd been going to add something about them going upstream to spawn but caught herself in time.

"Yes? You thought...?"

"Oh." What *had* she thought? "Uh, that perhaps we should cook them now. As warm as it is, won't they spoil?"

"As a matter of fact, no. They're on ice."

"Ice? Where'd you get *ice*?" He'd used the only chunk she knew of on her knee last night.

"From a glacier," he answered as if she should have guessed.

Blair's mind segued to her maps. As far as she could remember, the nearest glacier was over— "Two miles away and a thousand feet up?"

"More or less." Dominic shrugged. "A fairly easy climb, as a matter of fact."

If you were a mountain goat. Or a very determined man. "I give up. Gorp it is. Yours or mine?"

"How about 'ours'? I like the sound of that much better."

So did she, which irritated her no end.

As did the smile tugging at the corners of her mouth when she turned away. She and her movable parts would have to have a long talk about discipline.

It was a relief to rummage in her backpack for a few minutes. They were familiar things from a familiar world. She touched them like lodestones. Make a decision, Blair.

"Want something to drink?" Dom's voice intruded.

"Sure," she called, piling packets of assorted foodstuffs in her left hand. "Lemonade or an orange drink. If you don't have it, I do."

"It's okay. I have everything."

"That you do," she muttered under her breath, then sank back on her heels. Listen, Mackenzie, she scolded herself, if you don't stop this play on words, I'm going to zap some of your circuitry!

Thus warned, she rose to her feet, limped toward Dom and grimaced inwardly. Two large beach towels, his and hers, were spread seam to seam not a hair's breadth apart. Coupled with the expectant, predatory look in his eyes, it was altogether too pat and cozy. If push hadn't come to shove yet, it was well on its way. Or so Dominic might think.

"Nice," Blair commented lightly, then dumped her load like a dividing line in the middle. "How's that for a choice?"

"Great," he said dryly. With a rueful smile, Dom cocked an eyebrow in graceful surrender as he sat down, Indian-style, on his side of the boundary she'd imposed, then handed her a mug. "Plain water. I figured you'd choose what's best for you."

"I fully intend to." Blair hoped her remark held plenty of conviction on a more personal level as she followed his actions and tucked her heels under her thighs. She had positioned herself at the far edges of her towel so felt relatively secure. They might be face-to-face, but not side-by-side, where the odds of touching were all in his favor. One jump ahead; it was all she asked.

"Relax, Blair. I'm not going to pounce all over you."

Exasperation flickered briefly. He was reading her mind again. "I didn't think you would. Well . . . maybe," she admitted, grinning at his disbelieving expression. "But it's your fault. You make me feel defensive."

"Because I've made up my mind about you?"

"Because you're making up my mind for me!"

"All I want you to do is listen to your instincts."

"Don't you mean libido? Quit pushing, Dom."

"Am I? Really?"

She almost snorted in exasperation. "Oh, come *on*!"

"You ain't seen nothin' yet," he teased her, then frowned at her forbidding expression. "I'm sorry. You're right. It's no joking matter. I'm not laughing, Blair. What you think, how you feel, is paramount to me."

His voice deepened, as did the color in his eyes. "That may sound damned impossible, considering the short time we've known each other, but it expresses the situation accurately." His gaze darkened. "If you want to know the truth, I have a certain phobia about wasting time."

"You do?" There was that sinking feeling again. "Why?"

"Experience. Time is a commodity I've learned to value. It can work for you, but more often than not, it's a thief, robbing you of choice, opportunity, happiness. I won't risk it again." Almost angrily, he ripped open a package of dates, offered them to her, then helped himself to a handful.

Still blinking a little at his vehemence, Blair carefully chose the least personal of the questions racing around in her head. "How long have you been a veterinarian?"

He flicked her a look she couldn't read, although a trace of a smile softened his features. "Nine-and-a-half years."

Encouraged, she popped a date in her mouth. "Were you always a cat specialist?"

"No. For several years I had a regular practice."

"What made you change?" she asked, having only a hazy layman's grasp of his profession.

"I was tired of looking at the back end of cows."

His voice had held no significant inflection, and if she hadn't been looking at him, she would have missed the shadowed expression in his eyes. Her smile faded.

Instinctively she hesitated, willing him to amplify, knowing, without knowing how she knew, that the decision had involved, for whatever reason, an event of major proportions in his life.

Did she dare probe? Did she really want to know? Would knowing drag her in deeper than she already was? Yes, she decided. Yes, yes and yes. Yet the strength of her curiosity surely wasn't all that surprising considering the circumstances. And considering the breathtaking attraction that whispered from her body to his at the oddest moments. A dangerous admission, but an honest one. As was the need to know more of his background, which so far was a complete mystery.

But as one who placed such high value on her own privacy, how could she rationalize invading his?

Just once I wish I had the gall of my ex-mother-in-law, Blair thought, wiggling her bottom into a more comfortable position. Then all I'd do was ask. Chewing another date, she darted a quick glance at his face. What was stopping her from doing the same? Caution, she concluded. Cowardice. A fear of involvement. Or, more realistically, a mixture of all three.

She hated waffling. Also, it was about time she took an emotional step forward.

"I find that a little hard to believe," she commented quietly, breaking the small pool of silence. "What happened, Dominic?"

His hesitation was fractional, but she saw it and caught her breath, then slumped in relief as he smiled. It was going to be all right.

"I haven't thanked you, have I?"

"What for?"

"For letting your heart overrule your fear this morning."

"Oh." Her voice flattened. "You mean Brutus." It seemed she'd been premature. Rebuff, no matter how kindly put, was hard to take. She should have remembered that from her own experience and minded her own business. "Forget it. It was nothing."

"It was *something*," he contradicted her. "Not only courageous but generous as well, sunshine. You've made both of us your friends for life."

As if friends were what she wanted. "Thanks," she said dryly.

"It's the other way around. As you may have noticed, Brutus means a lot to me."

"I know," Blair answered with a sigh, turning her attention downward. She didn't trust the burning sensation behind her eyes.

"Look at me," he commanded her gently.

Reluctantly, almost defiantly, she did.

"You asked me a question and I skirted around the answer. My remark about cows earlier is a stock phrase I've used automatically for years when anyone got curious enough to ask why I specialized. But you didn't deserve that, and I apologize." A frown formed across his forehead. "I'm as private a person as you seem to be, and when I ask for openness from you, it's a hell of a note if I close up myself just because the subject is still sore around the edges."

He put out a huge hand and rested it on her knee, his gesture demonstrating a request for understanding. "I want to share not only the present and the future with you but the past as well. But I have to get around to telling it in my own way, okay?''

The warmth of his smile eased the lump in her chest. "Of course." Blair nodded, feeling an odd sense of peace. It was as if some invisible barrier had been crossed. She flashed him a tentatively teasing look. "Would it help to begin with the day your were born?" She was inordinately pleased when he laughed.

"It might. How about cleaning up here first, though. If you're through, that is." Dom's brows quirked in inquiry.

For the life of her, she couldn't remember what or how much she'd eaten. Nor did she care. "Sure. While we're at it, I think I'll move into some shade." More to the west now, the afternoon sun seemed focused on the small meadow with concentrated heat. Her shirt was stuck to her back, and from the waist down Blair felt fried alive under the thin denim of her jeans.

"Good idea." His grin reflected his agreement. "In fact—" Dom rose to his knees and began gathering up their debris "—I'm going to peel out of these heavy clothes."

"Also a good idea. I think I'll do the same," she responded, thinking in strong terms of a comb and lipstick.

The heat in the tent made Blair gasp. It had also cooked dry her peach shorts and tube top, so she slipped back into them, then concentrated some rapid attention to face and hair as she grappled with an inner sense of expectancy.

Within minutes, feeling outwardly cooler, she came out of the tent . . . and slowed to a stop.

Naked except for jogging shoes and indecently short running shorts, Dom stood looking thoughtfully down at his still blissfully oblivious pet.

Thank goodness he had his back turned. He was so gorgeous it made her teeth ache. Blair groaned silently in real anguish, face mirroring the stunned impact banging around in her nether regions as her eyes took in the visual reality of solid muscle, bone and smooth bronzed skin in the impossible dimensions of his splendid body. A body that could be hers for the asking.

She tried to swallow and couldn't. Blast the man! He was turning her into a heavy breather.

Move, feet! she commanded. And was grateful when *something* worked right as her toes inched forward.

Blair limped over to him, careful to keep her distance, forcing her gaze to focus on the dog. "Should he still be sound asleep?"

"I gave him something to keep him quiet awhile. Unfortunately, it won't last long. He's going to hurt for a couple of days."

"Oh, gosh. The trip downtrail tomorrow is going to be a little rough on him, isn't it?"

"We'll see." He turned to look at her, eyes skimming with potent approval over her lightly clad body until he came to the Technicolor horror surrounding her knee. With a muffled curse he swept her up into his arms, strode determinedly over to a rock, plunked her not too gently down and dropped to one knee, running skilled fingers over the tender area. "I could wring your stubborn neck. Why didn't you let me look at this earlier?"

"It wasn't necessary," Blair answered rather vaguely. Her attention was locked on the broad, sun-kissed breadth of his massive shoulders and the heat lightning that was streaking from the touch of his hands on her knee to lodge with terrible accuracy somewhere in her lower extremities. This time she groaned out loud.

Frowning gray eyes snapped upward. "Does that hurt?"

"Yes!" she lied. "Quit poking at it that way." She shoved his hands away and stood up. "Go play doctor with your dog and leave me alone."

Far from taking offense and evidently satisfied with his probing, Dominic laughed, swung his big body to one side and settled down on the ground next to her rock, drawing his legs up to anchor his wrists. "Truce, you testy, sweet-smelling wench. Just let me know if it kicks up any worse than it is. I may be able to help. And for Pete's sake, relax. Sit. I can't talk to you way up there."

Having no excuse she could voice, Blair sat.

"That's better. Now, where was I?"

She knew precisely but held her tongue. What or how much he told her was his decision.

Brutus chose that moment to snort, roll over, sigh and settle back down in a series of sonorous canine snuffles that made Dominic smile with affection. "That's right. Sleep it off," he encouraged the dog gruffly. "Good boy."

Hmph, Blair thought. Her fear of Brutus might be gone, but affection hadn't taken its place.

Dom swung his attention back to her. "He comes from mixed but sturdy stock, if you haven't already guessed."

"I'll bet there's an elephant in there somewhere."

He laughed. "Not that I know of. His great-granddaddy was my first patient. I think I was eight years old at the time."

"Really?"

"True. I grew up in a large farming community in the middle of Michigan. Both my grandfather and father were doctors, and up until old Tor caught his leg in a trap, that's what I had wanted to be."

"I take it your patient recovered," Blair said with a grin.

"Of course." Dominic managed to look properly offended. "From that point on, our house was filled with a steady procession of walking and flying wounded. Peg—my mother—suffered through dogs, cats, mice, rabbits, an owl." He chuckled low in his throat. "Even a bad-tempered skunk."

"Uh-oh." She could see it coming.

"Oh, yeah. You guessed it."

"I'll bet she loved you for that."

"She did. And still does. Anyway, I grew up, went to college, played a little football—"

"You did?" Blair's eyes lit up. She was an avid Seattle Seahawks football fan. "What position?"

"Guard."

With that build, what else? "I'll bet you were *formidable*." She gave the word its full-powered French pronunciation.

"Let's say adequate." Dom raised his eyebrows modestly.

"Did you ever consider turning pro?"

"It's not that easy, sunshine. You have to be asked."

"Don't be condescending. Were you?"

"Well...yes. But I had a different dream. So I turned them down, went straight into vet school, and by my final year, I was engaged and felt I had the world by the tail."

"Engaged?" The word rattled around in her head and curdled her stomach. Why was she so surprised? And so shaken?

Dominic's eyes grew reminiscent as, caught up in the past, he overlooked the faint traces of dismay on Blair's face. "Her name was Beth, and the rapport she had with animals was something to see." Admiration deepened the natural resonance of his voice. "We had great plans, she and I: nail down our degrees, steadily build up a combined practice and, after a couple of years, be in a firm enough financial position to marry. We took pride, in fact, in our practicality. But..." He paused and leaned forward so Blair could no longer see his face. "It didn't happen."

She held her breath, listening to the silent thudding of her heart, wanting to ask, not sure if she should, vitally conscious of Dominic's tension in the rigid set of his broad back.

"She died," he added softly, "two months before the wedding."

Blair's breath came out in a stricken sound of sympathy. "Oh, Dom. I'm so sorry. What happened?"

He turned set, sober eyes in her direction. "Carelessness, pure and simple."

Whose? Beth's? His? "I'm not sure I understand," she said delicately.

"Neither did I. Not then, not now." Dominic exhaled heavily, trapping the depth of his emotions inside. "Even after all these years, the *waste* of it galls me. It just shouldn't have happened."

She still didn't understand. "Was it an accident?"

"I suppose you could call it that, although no one labeled it as such. There'd been an anthrax outbreak that scared the living daylights out of two counties. She and I and every other vet for fifty miles around were working nonstop to isolate the animals, dispose of infected carcasses, and try to pin down the source. Somehow, whether through an unprotected cut on her hands or inhaling spores from tainted animal hair, she caught it. Before any of us realized what had happened, it was too late. All the penicillin or tetracycline in the world wouldn't have helped."

"How awful," Blair said softly, wanting badly to touch him, to cup her hand against the vital warmth of his face and smooth away the pain of his past. No wonder he had spoken of nightmares. Oh, Dom...

"It was a rough time," he said bluntly. "My dad had died six months earlier, and suddenly it seemed there was nothing to bank on anymore. Peg and I survived, but the world was a much darker place for a damnably long period."

He turned to look at her, and Blair felt some of the sorrow seep out of her own system as she recognized strongly fought for acceptance in the clear gray of his eyes. "Was that when you moved out to the West Coast?" she asked.

"No. I felt I owed it to...myself to continue with the practice. Actually, it was Peg who made the move first. She came out to visit friends one year and fell in love not only with the area but with a man. When he died unexpectedly, she suggested I join her. Since she's my only living relative, it was hard to turn her down. Besides, her arguments always pulled some weight." He grinned slightly. "Especially when she carried on about the unparalleled beauty of Puget Sound and the surrounding wilderness. Coupled with her cause was an avalanche of snapshots taken only on *sunny* days. Her tactics got me out here; one look convinced me to stay. Within weeks I'd not only sold my old practice but bought out the cat clinic, which just happened to be available at the right time. Once that was settled—" he shrugged a massive bare shoulder "—everything else fell into place."

"Then you're not sorry you made the move?"

"No, ma'am," he assured her solemnly. His gray eyes, well lit with devilish signals, swept over her body. "I've found exactly what I was looking for."

Blair's skin burned as if he'd touched her. "Sick cats?" she offered. And smiled weakly when he laughed.

"Are there really enough of them around to keep you busy?" Not only was she curious, but it kept the conversation on safer ground.

"*Too* busy, according to Peg. Although she should talk. She's on the run more than I am and doesn't have the excuse of being on call."

"On call?"

"Just like an M.D." His mouth curved again. "At the clinic. And just like an M.D., I don't make house calls. Although—" he leaned closer and she caught her breath "—there are exceptions. Where do you live, Blair?"

"Edmonds," she blurted.

"Well, how about that." His voice had taken on deep, sexy, satisfied tones. "I won't have to commute."

"Commute?"

"You know, go from city to city. In case you haven't guessed—" he moved a fraction closer and kissed her sunburned nose "—meet Edmonds's all-time favorite vet. I 'specialize,' my love, right on your delectable doorstep."

Eight

___

Blair came bolt upright on her rock and felt sure her mouth dropped open straight to her knees. This hormone-stirring, impossibly possessive man prowled through her peace of mind not only up here in the woods but all over her home turf as well? Consternation widened her eyes as the consequences implied by his words sank in. Backing her face out of reach of his mouth, she met the caught-the-canary look in his eyes. "You're kidding."

"I'm not."

Darn it! She cast an exasperated look around the meadow. She loved Edmonds. The heart of the vibrant little city, which was situated just north of Seattle, pulsed energetically along Puget Sound's shoreline before it flowed eastward, up and over the surrounding hills. Born and bred within its limits, Blair felt a bone-deep proprietary kinship, not only for the city itself but for all its warm and intelligent inhabitants. Until now. *Now* Dominic Masters dominated the scene.

"Ho-ly cats," she breathed, feeling the small-city atmosphere she adored grow slightly claustrophobic.

"My sentiments exactly." Dom grinned like the Cheshire strain of the species and looked so male and so smug, she could have thumped him. "I've never believed in fate," he added, his voice dropping to a husky rumble, "but I'm beginning to. We might have been separated by half the state. Instead—" He broke off, eyes narrowing. "My clinic's at the top of the hill near Five Corners. Where are you?"

Oh, gosh. Less than twenty blocks away. "At the *bottom* of the hill," Blair answered, sinking in the mires of inevitability. "A couple of blocks up from the ferry dock."

"What street?"

"Columbia Place," she sighed. He could, after all, find her in the phone book.

"I know where it is," he said slowly, pinpointing it precisely in his mind. "Wait a minute. That can't be right. The only thing there is a big, run-down building."

"It may have been at one time," she conceded. "But not anymore. Now it's a gallery."

"Uh-oh. As in 'art'?"

"Of course as in art. What other kind is there?"

"Shooting?" he suggested, looking hopeful.

"Very funny." It was not only her profession but her home he'd just slurred. She and her partners had worked themselves to the bone, to create a warm, welcoming atmosphere. The renovations had been all they'd hoped for.

"How long has it been since you've been by there? And what," she continued, "do you have against art?" She'd caught the flat inflection in his voice and her artistic defenses rose.

Dominic winced. "I have a feeling I've struck a nerve. You're an artist? Your work's on exhibit there?"

"How *did* you guess?"

"Take the dagger out of my chest and I'll tell you." Dom gave her a smile to melt glaciers as he placed a conciliatory hand on her arm.

Blair, however, was not about to be placated. "Kindly remove your hand, Mr. Masters," she ordered him. "Answer my questions."

"Easy, tiger." He ignored her command and smoothed her sensitized skin as if it were ruffled feathers. "I'm sorry if I was tactless. It was an innocent remark."

"Nothing you say or do is innocent," Blair grumbled, tracking the path of his fingers. Gooseflesh was popping out all over her body, and she was having trouble holding on to her indignation.

"*Now* who's throwing stones?" Dom managed to look both amused and offended as his fingers curved down around her wrist and captured her hand. "Let's start back at the beginning." He laced his fingers through hers. "Where do you live?"

"I told you." Blair's answer held less force than she intended. The heat of his palm pressing against hers had begun to capture large portions of her attention.

"Where you exhibit, yes. But not your home address."

"It's one and the same. I live above the gallery."

"In that—"

"If you say 'run-down' again, I'll slug you!" She tried to snatch her hand away, with no success.

"I stand corrected," he assured her solemnly. "Tell me about it...and you." His gaze fell to their joined hands, and he spread her slender fingers along the larger contours of his own. Even to her eyes, her hand looked protected—and right—against the rugged proportions of his deeply tanned palm. Tactile pleasures shivered up her arm, through her chest and lodged in her throat. For a moment, she couldn't speak.

"So," he mused into the silence. "There's more talent in these small hands than I first imagined." He raised his eyes to lock with hers. "Come on. Open up to me, Blair."

Sharing implied trust. Did he know what he was asking? Of course he did. And Dominic demanded no less than what he had offered her. It was neither wise nor safe to be open with someone of his...potential to affect her life. From the instant she'd leaped into his arms out of fear of his dog, he'd been making her feel and think all sorts of impossible things. Which couldn't be real. If she could equate it with a weekend bout with a mysterious bug, maybe...just maybe...she'd be able to keep some perspective until she was back in her own absorbing world.

Blair straightened her shoulders. The best defense was a strong offense. If truth be told, she was in sore need of both. "Oh, no, you don't." She yanked her hand from his. "Not a word about me until you answer my question. Why are you acting so slippery?"

"Me? Slippery?" His strong features registered wounded surprise. "I gave you my whole life's story."

He had, her sense of fairness conceded. It made her reticence a viable issue. But there was a definite wariness in those devastating eyes of his. She was as intuitive as he, and something was fishy besides their intended dinner. It might just give her an edge. Heaven knew she needed one, she thought crossly. When had he waffled? Oh, yes. Art. "You don't like art," she challenged him.

"Let's just say it's not something that ranks high on my list."

"Have you ever given it a chance?"

He rolled his eyes in remembrance. "I didn't, but Peg sure did."

"Your mother?"

"She's a culture nut. From the time I could toddle until my foot grew big enough to put down, she dragged me to one thing after the other. At least during concerts, I could either daydream or get caught up in the music. But galleries?'' He shrugged in apology but with the air of a man determined to tell the truth at whatever cost. "Uh-uh. I was bored out of my gourd."

He couldn't have struck a more responsive chord if he tried. Far from being offended, Blair half turned to him, eyes sparkling and flooded with zeal. "But that's just it, Dom! Far too many of them *do* project a stuffy, intimidating atmosphere, and that's exactly what we were determined to avoid!" She paused to catch her breath. "Wait till you see it," she went on eagerly, unaware that she'd just shot herself and her inner arguments in the foot and was willingly giving them a future out of the mountains. "It's alive, filled with enormous activity, sound, creativity. We were determined— Hey!"

Blair's voice rose an octave and she nearly jumped out of her skin as a cold, wet nose preceded Brutus's bony head as he wedged it across her bare thighs and tried to climb into her lap. "Hold it, you big moose!" she yelped, grabbing a fistful of fur to keep her balance. "What do you think you're doing?"

Dominic broke out in laughter. "Didn't I tell you he loved you?"

"It's not me he wants," Blair sniffed. "Look at his eyes. He's casting those soulful looks at you."

"Whose lap is he in?"

"That's entirely beside the point," she said loftily. Her gaze caught the flash of white bandage on the dog's leg. "Dom! Did you see that? I think he put some weight on his foot."

"Quit worrying. He'll be fine in a couple of days. You have my word on it." Dominic leaned forward. "I know what I *didn't* see."

He spoke so gently, Blair turned her head to look at him. He was pleased, obviously, his look as warm as the hand he placed on her shoulder. He answered her unspoken question with one of his own. "Where's the fear, Blair?"

"Fear?" Did he mean the panicky feeling she had when he touched her like that or... Her gaze dropped to Brutus, who cocked lopsided ears and gave her a sappy grin. "Oh, you mean him."

Wound in a more dramatic evolution of emotions, thanks to Dominic, she'd barely noted her apprehension passing. She opened her mouth, closed it, then opened it again. And tilted her chin stubbornly. "I still think he's so ugly he ought to be banned."

"But...?" Dom prompted her.

Blair took a deep breath. "You're right," she conceded. "I...don't know where it went, but it's gone."

"You have to face fear to conquer it."

"Is that a fact?" She felt a faint flicker of irritation. As if she didn't know, having faced and flattened a few of them in order to call her life her own. "Don't preach, Dominic."

His laugh exploded. "Preach? That's the first time I've ever been accused of that! Usually, I'm the preachee."

Her glance swept from his beard-shadowed face down over his massive bronzed chest to the indecently stretched shorts, where it seemed to get snagged before she dragged it back up to the breath-catching challenge of his eyes. He was the stuff of a sermon or two, all right—Temptation incarnate! "I don't doubt that for a minute," she snapped, hoping she had the willpower to resist.

"Feisty, feisty." He chuckled. "By the way, who's the 'we' you mentioned in the same breath as the gallery?"

Good grief. He changed gears like an eight-wheeler. "My partners."

"Male? Female?"

"Not quite half and half."

"I'm pulling teeth here, lady." Frustrated, he ran a hand through his hair. "Instead of crinkling that cute nose of yours, how about helping me out?"

"I'm sorry," she said, and meant it. He was presumptuous, inordinately confident, with an aura of masculine dominance, and it was about time he knew who she was and what she would and would not stand for...as long as he kept his hands to himself. When he touched her, things started to get a little scrambled. An understatement if she ever heard one. "I'm not used to talking about myself," she added, easing the death grip she had on Brutus's wrinkly neck. "Tell you what." Blair used her best bargaining tone. "You help me, then I'll help you."

Dom's dark brows climbed. "This could get interesting. What is it you want me to do?"

"Nothing much, so don't get your hopes up."

"That's not all that's—"

"Get this two-ton derelict off my lap!"

His earthy chuckle made the ground shake. "Shucks, ma'am. Is that all? Just tell him to move."

"Come on, Dominic. He won't do what I tell him."

"Wanna bet?"

She thought about that for a minute. The dog *had* come off that rock in the stream at her command. "I guess not."

"Wise choice. You'd lose. Speaking of betting." His eyes danced with mischief. "How are you at...high-stakes games?"

Ha! Sexual Pursuit, no doubt. "Deadly." She kept her gaze cool and level and as composed as she could, considering the chaos going on inside. *Damn* her fertile imagination.

Dom's laugh gave her good marks for outbluffing. "We'll have to see how well you do when the stakes are really...a challenge," he suggested with a comic leer. "But right now, we have a bargain. Brutus, old boy, it looks like you'll have to give the lady some room. Tell him to move, sunshine, then to go lie down. Use that firm, no-nonsense tone you reserve for me."

With a flash of her eyes at the man, Blair spoke to the dog.

With a heartbroken sigh, Brutus gave her a look sad enough to wring tears from a rock, lumbered to his feet and, dragging a woebegone tail, moved half a yard away to collapse in a shaggy black heap, his manner reproachful.

Blair, however, was delighted. "He did it!" By his instant obedience, the dog had given her the upper hand, and with control there *was* nothing to fear, she realized, riding on a crest of euphoria. "Well! Maybe he's not so ugly after all."

Dom threw his head back and roared with laughter.

Realizing what she'd just said, she grinned weakly. "I guess I—"

"Got carried away?" Dominic suggested, folding her in his great arms and giving her a hug any bear would envy. "Oh, my darlin' girl," he told her with deep masculine relish, "feel free anytime. It's good for my soul."

"Mmmpff," Blair protested, finding her face suddenly pressed into his broad chest. She groaned inwardly. Even in laughter this wasn't a safe place to be! But her eyelashes had tangled in the sparse drift of dark hair delineating his massive contours. Her nose, her mouth, trapped in potent intimacy, flared at the virile scent, the taste of his sun-slick skin, and her blood, in swift reaction, beat with a frenzy of thunder in her ears. Her world seemed to spin, to tip on its axis, and she stiffened, fighting the urge to cling.

Then just as her will was weakening, his arms began to loosen. She eased away, letting him slip from her fingers as his hand tilted her chin upward. No words would come, and she could only stare at him.

"It's always there, isn't it? The chemistry."

His voice, low and poignant, echoed clear through her body. How could she lie when the rough-textured surface of his thumbs had discovered the panicky pulse at the base of her throat? She nodded, lost in the drama of his eyes.

"Don't kid yourself that it's going to diminish," he warned her huskily. "Not when something is as right as I know this is."

"You have a one-track mind." Blair struggled to sound firm. "And don't take that as a compliment."

His own voice, rich and lazy, held anything but concern. "I've been accused of worse. While we're listing my attributes, there's something else you need to know." His hands stilled to hold her more firmly, and his eyes and tone sobered, and she caught herself holding her breath.

"I seldom take no for an answer, and I rarely change my mind."

The words, with their undercurrent of promise, seemed to squeeze a warning fist around her heart. "Dominic, don't! You have no idea who I am or anything about me!" Her voice, at first as low as his, held a rising thread of warning. She was not a pushover. Not any longer.

"I know enough to get by. The rest we're going to work on in a minute. Right now, however—" his smile resurfaced, easing the bold lines of his mouth "—I have another problem."

If that was a ploy to ease her guard, he'd made a tactical error. For some reason, his problems always caused *her* problems. She regarded him warily, not liking the look in his eyes. However reluctantly, she had to ask. "What's that?"

"I haven't kissed you for hours," he murmured, slowly narrowing the small space between them.

The mouth she should have kept closed went dry. Instinctively, Blair pulled back...against the swift surge in her heart, her breasts, her loins. Remember the tent! she thought wildly. You lost control then; you'll do it again! "Don't!" she gasped, and Dominic froze in midmotion.

"What's wrong?"

What could she say? That if he kissed her the way he'd kissed her before, she'd have him down on the ground and out of his shorts in nothing flat? While not quite the truth, it was close enough to make her break out in hives.

Blair agonized briefly. Not that the idea didn't hold merit. Dominic in the buff would be— She shuddered and blocked the image out of her mind.

"Blair, what's the matter? You look a little strange."

Is that what they called sexual suppression these days? she thought. "Oh, well, uh..." More in a bid for time than anything else, she raised her hand to smooth her fingers against his beard.

"So that's it." His expression brightened.

Huh? She looked around, wondering where rescue had come from.

"It's the beard."

Her eyes snapped back to his. Beard?

"It bothers you, doesn't it?"

"Well, I..."

"You don't like it."

Personally, she thought it got in the way, but she'd never dream of saying so. "Oh, well, I..."

"Prefer a clean-shaven male?" Dom's eyes fairly danced. "Good. I'm a bare-skin man myself."

"Oh, but—"

"It's okay, dark eyes. You haven't hurt my feelings. I grew it on a whim in the first place. So it's coming off."

The man was amazing! A bewilderment of contradictions. Dominating, accommodating, so macho he made her mad, yet so perceptive he made her melt. She'd never known anyone like him. "If you say so," she said, wondering why she was defending the thing in the first place. Because with it gone, with Dominic smooth-jawed, she'd be left in no doubt as to the stubbornness of his hidden chin? Blair sighed. She'd face that when she had to. Meanwhile, she could breathe a little easier. The issue had taken her out of immediate trouble.

But his hands came up to frame her face and she was forced to meet his eyes. Oh, gosh. If there was any dancing going on in them now, it was to a slow, sensual tango. Without missing a beat, her heart rate stepped straight into the tempo.

"That's a promise, sweetheart. I'll shave it off especially for tonight."

Tonight? What was special about *tonight*?

"However insignificant," he went on with a solemnly sexy smile, "I want *nothing* to come between us. Ever."

Still tangled in thoughts of "tonight," Blair barely heard. What did he have in mind, as if she didn't know. And she was weakening. *Contemplating...!* If he so much as tried again—she made herself complete the thought—she'd probably fall all over her feet to oblige him.

Make a stand while you still can, Blair. Physically and emotionally, she rose to her feet.

For once, she caught him off guard. "Wait a minute. Where are you going?"

"To get something to drink," she said, improvising. "I'm thirsty."

In one masterful motion, he stood also, stretched like a lazy lion, eyed her as if she were dinner and threw a huge arm around her shoulders. "Come to think of it, so am I. What's your pleasure this time, darlin'?"

Not you, she thought with an unequal mix of regret and resolve. It *can't* be you. My life would never be the same.

Oh, Blair, she thought. Would that be so bad?

The lament brought her up short for several beats as she envisioned Dominic in her bed, in her soul, in her body. Her breath caught painfully in her chest. Whether Dom sensed something or not, his arm tightened, bringing her securely against the hard, lean planes of his side. Her knee had stiffened, making her barefooted gait uneven, and Blair bit her lip as he easily adjusted the lithe motion of his stride to match hers.

He was so big, this man. So male. Her fingers trembled. All around them rose the rich aroma, the somnolent sounds, of a soft summer afternoon. Beneath her feet the meadow grass was sun-warmed, springy with vibrant life. But Blair's mind, her senses, the surface of her skin, burned with the awareness, the heat of his burnished arm, his hand cupped possessively around her sensitized shoulder, the incidental contact of his thigh brushing against hers as they walked slowly toward their campsite. She felt stifled, and suddenly it all seemed . . . too much.

On the pretext of picking one of the pale blue flowers, Blair ducked out and away from the intimidating intimacy of his touch and bent low. The stem snapped sweetly under the pressure of her fingers, and she rose, focusing on the fragile petals, the pale golden center.

"Blair, what'll it be?"

She raised her head reluctantly. That's right. He'd asked her a question earlier, and she had to think hard before she could remember what it was. "Oh . . . plain water."

"Plain and simple it is," he agreed.

"If only it were," she murmured under her breath as she watched him scoop up a bucket and head for the stream.

The late-afternoon sun slanted shifting shadows across the massive slope of his shoulders. In helpless fascination, Blair followed the play of his muscular coordination as he curved at the waist, swept a strong arm downward in a deep arc. He straightened and turned, flashing her a quick smile of accomplishment as he headed back toward her. He was . . . magnificent.

She'd give anything to capture him on canvas! For the first time in almost eight years, Blair cursed her switch to soft sculpture. She hadn't touched a brush seriously since then. Even if she had, she admitted, she'd never do him justice.

But Barney could! Her face lit. She could almost *see* his swift, powered strokes take form on canvas. Blair took an excited breath. Her theme—Spatial Dimensions! *Dom's* dimensions—life-size! The correlation in concepts almost made her dizzy. What if...

"Now, what's put that dazzling gleam in those dark eyes, Ms. Mackenzie? Anticipation of coming events, I hope."

"Yes!" she almost crowed, missing his point entirely. "Dom! Have you ever done any modeling?"

"Modeling?" Surprise gave way to the sexiest smile she'd ever seen. "Well, I'll be a son of a gun! You mean you want to scope out my...er, muscles?"

"Yes...I mean, no!" she amended hastily as he took a quick step forward. "That is—oh, darn it, Dominic!" The words scrambled themselves in her head. She took a breath and raised her chin. "As a matter of fact, I *would* like you to pose. With that physique, you'd be perfect for a nude study."

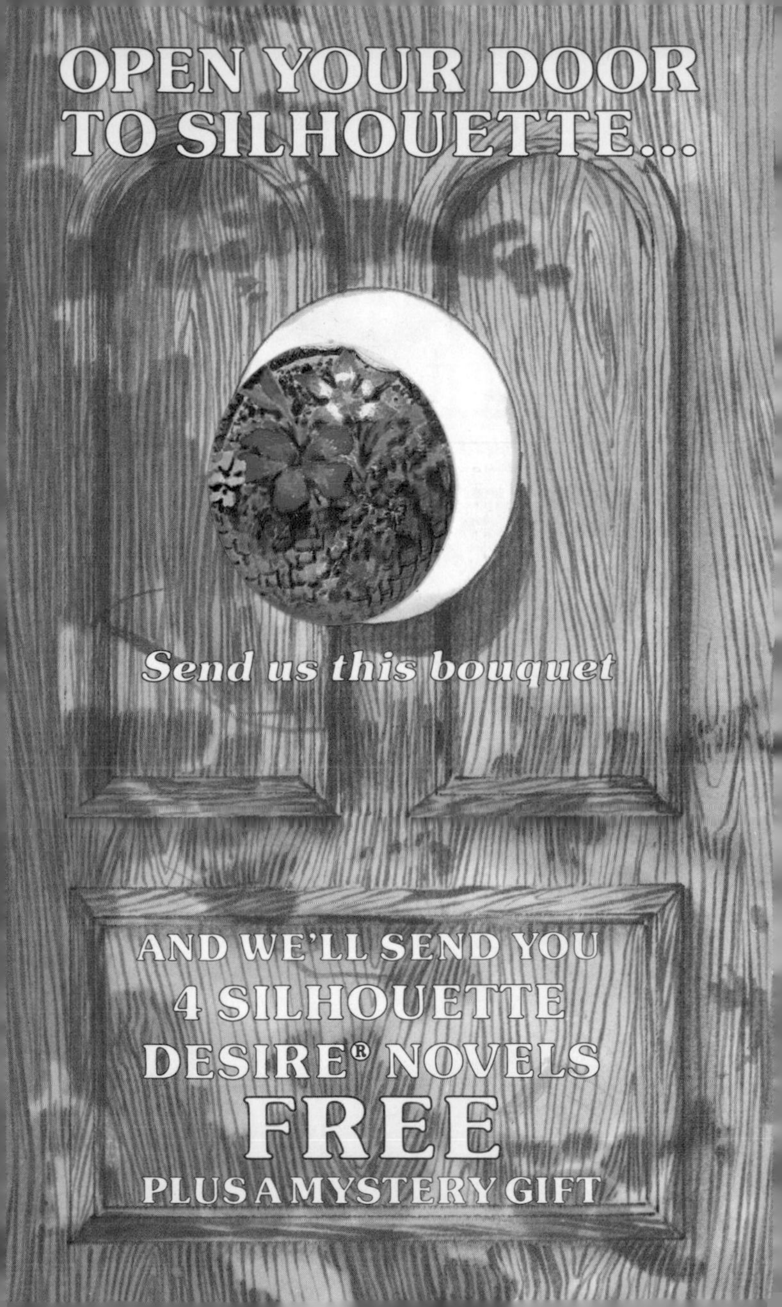

OPEN YOUR DOOR
TO SILHOUETTE...
Send us this bouquet
AND WE'LL SEND YOU
4 SILHOUETTE
DESIRE® NOVELS
FREE
PLUS A MYSTERY GIFT

NOW THAT THE DOOR IS OPEN . . .
**Peel off the bouquet and send it on the postpaid
order card to receive:**

4 FREE BOOKS
from

Silhouette ❤ Desire®

And a mystery gift as an extra bonus!

MONEY-SAVING HOME DELIVERY!

Once you receive your 4 FREE books and gift, you'll be able
to open your door to more great romance reading month after
month. Enjoy the convenience of previewing 6 brand-new
books every month delivered right to your home months
before they appear in stores. Each book is yours for only
$2.25—.25¢ less than the retail price, plus .69¢ postage and
handling per shipment.

NO-RISK GUARANTEE!

—There's no obligation to buy—and the free books and gift
are yours to keep forever.
—You pay the lowest price possible and receive books
months before they appear in stores.
—You may end your subscription anytime—just write and
let us know.

**RETURN THE POSTPAID ORDER CARD TODAY AND
OPEN YOUR DOOR TO THESE 4 EXCITING LOVE-
FILLED NOVELS. THEY ARE YOURS ABSOLUTELY
FREE ALONG WITH YOUR MYSTERY GIFT.**

Nine

"What?" His bellow of disbelief sloshed water over the edge of the pail, flushed a bevy of camp robbers out of the trees, and brought Brutus to his feet in a single bound.

Ohmigosh! What had she said? "I didn't mean for *me*!" Blair gasped. "I meant—"

Dom dropped to his knees and reached for her forehead. "You've got to get out of the sun," he rumbled solicitously. "You're having a heat stroke!"

"Let me explain!"

"Okay," he said several sensual decibels lower. "You want me to pose."

Blair unclenched her fists. "Well . . . yes."

"In the nude?" He raised his eyebrows suggestively.

She ignored his exhibition. "Sure, if Barney agrees."

"Barney?" Dom's brows snapped together.

"An artist. The one I hope will do your portrait," she answered quickly. "My partner."

"Why not you?"

"I don't have the skill. He does. You'd like his work, Dominic. He's genuinely talented." Blair paused for a moment, then played her trump card. "He's even been hung internationally."

"And still functions? He must have one strong neck! Sorry, sweetheart. The answer is no."

"Why not?"

"Would *you* pose in the nude?"

"Well—"

"I thought not. Case closed. But, at least it's brought us full circle."

The steel in his eyes, the grim line of his mouth, warned her not to push. "What's that supposed to mean?" If she sounded disgruntled, that was too bad. It had been a *stunning* idea.

"We're back to talking about the gallery."

"I thought you weren't interested."

"It doesn't turn me on like you do, no. But I have a gut feeling if I hear about it, I'll learn more about you. Who are the rest of your partners, besides the benighted Barney? What's his last name, by the way?"

"Richardson. I'd be careful about calling him names. He outweighs you by at least a hundred pounds."

Dom grimaced. "What is he . . . a sumo wrestler? Sounds like my kind of guy."

"With *my* luck, you'd end up best of friends."

"Why not? I'm easy to like. Who else? Come on, Blair. Share yourself with me."

That plea, she sighed inwardly, was already fixed deep in her mind and her lower extremities. "There's five more: Selena Marshall, Georgio DeSantis, Steven Bellflower, Felicity Tanaguchi, and Shad Fitzpatrick."

"Whew. A mixed bag. Do they all paint?"

"Heavens no. Selena produces porcelain and pottery between sprouting offspring."

Dominic's eyes narrowed. "Did I hear right?"

"She's working on her fourth, so takes some kidding."

"Mmm. How do *you* feel about ba—"

"Georgio," Blair plowed on swiftly, "is our resident glassblower and specializes with Mount Saint Helens ash."

"Do tell."

"I'm trying," she said severely. "Then there's Steven, who is a jeweler *extraordinaire*. His studio is also incorporated in the gallery."

"Four down, three to go."

"Shall I stop?" Her eyes flared.

"By no means. I'm all ears."

"So I noticed," she said sweetly, and went on without missing a beat, "Felicity does some of the most delicate and complex batiks I've ever seen."

"And . . . what's his name . . . Shag?"

"Shag," Blair confirmed, affection softening her voice. "He's my favorite."

"Oh?" Dom's tone grew slightly suspicious. "What's *his* forte that has that charmed note tripping past your tongue?"

Fitzpatrick was sixty-five, if he was a day, and reminded Blair of her father. Dominic, she decided, needed a good dig in his presumptuous ego. "He sculpts," she breathed, larding as much awe as she thought she could get away with into her voice.

"In other words, the guy's a chiseler and chips rocks for a living."

Blair bit back a bubble of laughter. Dominic, she discovered, was even more intriguing when he bristled. It was all she could do to keep a straight face as she shrugged. "He's *very* good."

"I intend to be a lot better," he muttered not quite low enough for her to miss. Then his voice rose as his gaze changed from one of aggression to masculine determination. "So now we've finally come around to you, haven't we?"

"It rather looks that way, doesn't it?" She cocked her head to look downward. "What do you intend doing with that bucket, by the way?"

His glance dropped to his hand. "Darned if it hadn't skipped my mind. Are you still thirsty? If not—" he rose to his feet "—I'll give this to Brutus and get us some wine. It might help you relax before I start dinner."

"Wine?" She looked at him, over at his backpack, then rolled her eyes. "Don't tell me; let me guess."

It was Dom's turn to shrug. "I do like those creature comforts." He smiled. "Now, go sit down, Blair. You've been standing on that leg too long."

"Is that an order, Mr. Masters, or a request?"

"Merely a professional observation," he intoned piously, then spoiled the effect as he leaned down, kissed her challenging eyes and straightened. "One mug of wine coming up in a hurry. For medical purposes, of course."

"Oh, of course," Blair echoed. It took an effort to hide a smile.

She watched him stride away. With anyone else—her ex-husband came to mind briefly—one-upmanship would have had her grinding her teeth. With Dominic, it was different. Though he kept her off balance, she found herself struggling as much with laughter as she did for advantage.

It was strange, but even in verbal victory, he made her feel warm, protected...cherished. Blair limped slowly into some shade and sank to the soft grass, following Dom's movements as he dropped to one knee and ministered to his dog.

He has such knowledgeable hands, she mused reluctantly. Skilled, sure, sensitive. Like the man himself.

Her breath caught. He was getting to her too deeply. It was long past time to explain her life to him in full detail. Aside from their shared penchant for hiking alone in the wilderness—and the strong mutual flare-up of physical response—they had little in common, much less ground for compatibility in areas of prime importance.

Cats and dogs, for instance. Blair glanced up in time to see the black brute lumber to his feet. Or boats bobbing around in heavy seas. *Her* feet were solidly grounded on terra firma, her whole perspective narrowed to the thrill, the challenge of artistic creativity, the whole idea of which left him cold. So, aside from physical chemistry, what was there to build on?

"Here you go, sunshine."

She turned her head away from the fascinating sight of Brutus slopping his way to the bottom of the bucket and reached automatically for the mug Dom extended. "White, I presume," she commented without looking as Dominic dropped down beside her, stretching his long, muscular legs out almost under her nose. Where, she wondered, was she going to put her own legs? If she so much as straightened her toes, she'd brush bare skin against his. All ten pink-tinted appendages flexed deep into the grass. Don't you try it, she told them, and dug deeper.

"White wine it is. With a taste almost as miraculous as your mouth." Dom's smile reached far into his eyes. "*Salud*, sweetheart," he added, voice soft and confident. "Here's to a long and lusty love affair."

Blair almost strangled getting the wine off her lips and back in the mug. She'd pour it into the ground before she'd drink to that. Her face burned as bright as the white-knuckled grip on her cup as she envisioned becoming the talk of the center of town. Good grief! What would her partners think?

An instant picture of that entire tempestuous tribe shouting, "Hey! Go for it!" popped into her head. Wrong question, she decided. There'd be no help there. She was alone in this battle of wills just as she'd been in the one with Greg and his mother. She set her jaw. So be it. "No!"

"No? You don't like the taste?"

Blair ground her teeth. "No long, no lusty, no love, and *no affair*! For once in your life, Dominic Masters, you're going to take no for an answer!"

"Like hell," he said even more gently than he had spoken before.

"Will you listen to me!" Blair slapped the cup down on the ground, came to her feet and whirled to face him. For once, she was taller than he, and she took advantage of it, hand on hips, face glowering. "My career, the gallery, what I choose to do with my life, takes up twenty-four hours of every day, three hundred and sixty-five days of the year! Do I make myself clear?" Smoke, she decided, must be coming out of her ears.

"Why?" he asked mildly.

"*Why?* Because I choose it, *that's* why."

"What about friends?"

"My partners *are* my friends."

"I meant outside the gallery."

Maggie Cappelini sprang to her mind. Blair closed her mouth before the name could escape. Maggie was not only extremely well known in the community; she was young at heart and, for all Blair knew, a dyed-in-the-wool matchmaker. All she needed was for the two of them to get their heads together and talk. No other name came forward instantly, so she shrugged. It was none of his business, actually. She said so.

"Sure it is. How else can we—"

"Don't even say it!"

"—Get to be friends?" he finished blandly.

"Friends? Don't flash that innocent look at me! What is this, a masterly switch in tactics?" she mocked, holding tight to her temper.

"Merely a Masters maxim. Friends first; lovers second."

"Quit trying to be cute! I'm serious."

"So am I." He sat up, voice coaxing. "Come on, Blair. Sit down, sip some wine, relax, and we'll talk. Or, rather..."

He smiled with enough charm to sizzle an iceberg. "You talk, and I'll listen. No more pressure. I promise."

"Until next time," she grumbled. But quick to anger, quicker to cool and needing to set him straight, she bent, picked up her mug and dropped back down to sit a safe three feet away, unconsciously rubbing at the ache in her knee.

Dominic frowned, but he wisely kept still and lounged back on an elbow, reflecting total masculine interest. "Fire at will, sunshine."

"Don't tempt me," she said dryly.

"A challenge we'll go into at length . . . later," he promised her smoothly. "Why did you imply you hadn't the talent when the topic of my . . . er, physical attributes came up? A touch of maidenly modesty due to subject matter, or modesty regarding your skill?"

"Ha! I've done so many nudes, I'm immune," she lied, looking him right in the eye. "But I haven't painted in years."

For once, he looked mystified. "You said you not only live in but also work at the gallery. And you're an artist. So what medium?"

"Soft sculpture. More recently I've done quite a few projects in stained glass. I also," she added to fully make her point, "am the managing director. With all three, I'm kept completely occupied."

"We'll get to that in a minute. Explain soft sculpture."

Her smile was spontaneous. "That's a tall order."

"Try me."

Not if she could help it! Blair took a fortifying sip of wine. "It includes anything from petit point to fabricated figures ten feet tall. Weaving, basketry, stitched and padded wall hangings. I use fabric, yarn, malleable plastic—any material that's bendable, in fact. There're no limitations other than my imagination." She added in captivating candor, "Since I have a good one, I never lack for ideas."

"I'll *bet* you don't." Dom chuckled. "As a matter of fact, neither do I. Which we'll also get to in a minute. Meanwhile, how did you get into stained glass?"

"By design," she said, paying him back with a private little play on words. Make him ask.

When he did, she relented. "I was working on a large wall hanging when a customer saw it. He wanted it, not as it was but as a window in his home. *Voilà!* I went from fabric to glass."

"A tribute to your talent," he said. "How did you end up as manager?"

"A penchant for details," she said promptly, pleased at his comment, "and the ability to twist arms without hurting, I guess. Actually—" she smiled slightly, remembering "—I was more or less railroaded into it when everyone learned I could add."

"Everyone meaning your partners, I take it. Sounds like you've known them for a long time."

Blair nodded. "Since college. That's where most of us met, schemed and dreamed grandiose dreams."

"Not all of that came true though, I take it."

It was her turn to look confused. "What do you mean? The gallery's a reality."

"Somewhere in that brief biography, there's a marriage and a divorce."

Blair looked at him coldly. "You don't pull your punches, do you?"

"Not if it helps to clear the air. I want to understand you, where you're coming from." He paused. "So I can join you. Wherever that is. Was your husband an artist, too?"

The idea was so ludicrous, it wiped out the first part of his statement. "Hardly," she said sardonically. "Success and politics are his only priorities."

Dominic sat up in surprise, his powerful shoulders hunching forward. "He's a politician?"

Blair shook her head, mahogany curls dancing in the sunlight. "No, that's not his style. He owns a couple of local newspapers and wheels and deals through the power of the press. Media manipulation at its best. Or worst."

Dominic's features hardened. "How did you ever get tangled up with someone like him?"

"Through my own stupidity." Blair ran a slender finger around the rim of her mug. Dominic might as well hear it all. Her choices, the ironclad control of her life-style, were bound up intrinsically with the mistakes in her past. Mistakes, she vowed silently, she'd never make again. She took a deep breath, tucked her legs up Indian-style and looked at him, dark eyes serious. "I met him when he was a guest speaker in a business class I took after graduation. He was...dynamic." She frowned, remembering. "I was swept off my feet by blond, tall, tanned charm and was too starry-eyed to question whether or not we thought alike."

"What happened?"

Blair hesitated, then shrugged. "I discovered fairly quickly that our goals in life simply weren't the same. Greg is one of those intensely competitive people. His whole life was—and still is—wrapped up almost exclusively in his newspapers. What I didn't realize was that he expected me to be equally committed. Almost before I knew it, I was at a desk in front of a computer six days a week and wishing I'd taken an assertiveness class as well."

"So you did work for him."

"Of course. We were a *team*," she said, her voice tinged with mockery.

"And your own career?"

"Put on hold."

Dominic's eyes darkened to slate as his voice dropped to a low, soft rumble. "That must have hurt like hell."

"It did, especially at first. Then I came to realize that because of the kind of work he does, he tends to see things in black and white, while I, as an artist, see things in color. It helped to put things in perspective and my priorities in order. When I told him I was quitting to help put together the gallery, our relationship collapsed. Art, as far as Greg is concerned, is okay as a hobby, but not something to take seriously, much less try to make a living with.''

His gaze held hers for a long unwavering moment. ''I could use a drink,'' he finally said quietly, picked up his mug, glanced at hers, and frowned. ''I'll be right back.''

I could use one myself, Blair thought, wondering what Dominic was thinking. She looked down, was a little surprised to find her cup nearly full and took a long, slow swallow.

Before she was finished he was back, dropping down inches away from her and fixing her again with the intensity of his eyes. ''How long did you take it, Blair?''

Ah. They weren't through with it yet. Somehow, she hadn't thought so. ''I stuck tight for a little over a year. To tell you the truth, I might have stayed—tried—longer, but Bea was the clincher.''

''Bea?''

Blair glanced at him, deliberating. She knew Dom had a special relationship with his mother, and she suspected she might hit a sensitive nerve with what she was about to say. But he'd asked. And the trauma she'd been through was enough to color her feelings the rest of her days. She opted for candor. ''Greg's mother. *Another* unpleasant surprise.''

''In what way?'' Dominic's alert gaze narrowed in intensity.

Blair grimaced. ''Are you sure you want to hear this?''

''Now more than ever,'' he answered with a look she couldn't decipher. ''What did she have to do with your marriage?''

She almost snorted. ''Quite a lot, as it turned out. While whirling me off my gullible feet, Greg somehow forgot to mention that we would live with her. Every penny we made, you see, had to be poured back into the paper. So I was not only free labor but a buffer to keep Bea from demanding so much of his time."

Blair hesitated, ruminating a bit, very aware she had Dominic's total attention. "In her eyes," she continued, "Greg could do no wrong. But because our courtship was so fast, I was as much of a shock to her as she was to me. And we were as much alike as oil and water."

She gave him a look of amusement. "To tell you the truth, I was a menace in the kitchen, pulled flowers instead of weeds and preferred sketching to housework on my one day off. Bea was . . ."

"Was what, Blair?"

She shrugged. "Rigid in her outlook, took Greg's side in every argument and never let me forget there was only one right way to do things—hers."

"I think I get the picture." Dominic's voice was low, abstracted, and held a note of another emotion she couldn't identify.

"You're quicker than I was." Blair sighed. "It took me more than a year before I reached a point of suffocation strong enough to file for divorce." She laughed shortly. "They *still* can't believe I meant it."

Dom's features tensed as he narrowed his eyes. "Are you seeing them—*him*—now?" His voice held all the tonal qualities of a very primitive man whose hearth and home were at risk. In fact, she thought with a surprised feminine instinct, he sounded . . . jealous. Her eyes met his squarely.

"Not if I can help it," she retorted in a voice as positive as she could make it. "Every darned time they call, I'm tempted to tear out my hair. It's one of the reasons I came up—" She stopped short.

"I see. Then I take it you're not still in love with him?"

"No!" Blair was genuinely shocked. "What ever gave you that idea?"

"Nothing. I don't know." His clear gray gaze searched hers as if verification lay somewhere in her eyes. "I...guess I just needed to hear you say it."

Dominic in need of assurance? Her glance swept over his huge solid body and as quickly returned to his face. She understood how it was when emotions were involved. His touched her. Deeply. "It's all ancient history," she answered with relative composure. Then spoiled the effect as she shivered.

Something Dominic didn't miss. His mouth thinned. "This is the last time you'll *ever* need to escape from the past, Blair. Count on it."

"You're reading reactions that aren't there." She got to her feet. "The breeze has kicked up and I'm getting chilled."

It was true, she'd discovered. The shade they'd been in had long since deepened to late-afternoon shadows. Combined with wind that seemed straight off the glaciers, there'd been a quick drop in temperature. A valid excuse for gooseflesh and wrapping herself in the armor of more clothing. She hoped he'd do the same.

Even more important was *emotional* distancing. The recapitulation of a low point in her life had left her feeling a little raw, which she needed to deal with privately.

Dominic rose to move up behind her. "Let me warm you," he murmured, wrapping his arms around her.

She stood absolutely still, feeling the heat of his body singe the full length of her back, fighting the urge to turn, to lift herself up and into him as she'd done before. "Let me go, Dom," she murmured. "Please. Let me go."

His massive arms tightened, then, miraculously, loosened. He gently turned her around, cupping her face with his huge hands. "Momentarily, and only because you've asked. I think I understand. You need a little space between the past and the present." His smile was brief and self-derogatory.

"Sometimes my timing is terrible. You'll have to help me work on that, okay?"

She nodded, grateful for his understanding. He was as perceptive as he was generous. She clenched her hands, keeping them at her sides. "I'll . . . be back."

"I'll be here," he promised softly, making it sound like a vow. "I think . . . maybe an early dinner, don't you?"

"Yes," she answered without hesitation, feeling deep in her soul she was agreeing to much more than was said. Swift hidden currents flowed through her bloodstream as, dark eyes wide, she smiled briefly, touched his arm as if in promise, then turned and limped away.

Ten

Somewhere there had to be a glorious sunset, Blair mused as she huddled more securely into the warmth of her down-filled jacket. Streaks of crimson slashed across the evening sky, casting pink-tinged tones over the meadow, deepening shadows, rivaling the campfire in color.

Holding her hands out to the fire's heat, Blair eased back down to the ground, grateful for Dominic's "posh pile of rocks," which kept the main force of the freshening wind from reaching her. The night was going to be cold.

Yet dusk, far from the intrusion of civilization, held a certain expectancy that never failed to move her. As nature's day shift settled into sleep, nightbirds woke and became watchful; bats swept in swift formations from dark space to darker place; small animals, made bold by the failing light, rustled through the underbrush foraging for food. The forest was never still; life stirred, shifted, evolved.

Much like human emotions, she thought, remembering the closeness she and Dom had shared scant hours ago. But from the moment she had reappeared, dressed once more in hiking boots, jeans and long-sleeved shirt, Dominic had dropped the teasing intimacy that had so characterized their conversations. She should be grateful. Perversely, she missed it.

Not that she could vocally fault his attitude. As the day had rapidly diminished, and all through their superb trout dinner, he'd been so skillfully *pleasant* it had set her teeth on edge.

Shouldn't she have welcomed the distancing? Been pleased with the tact he had shown in giving her breathing space?

That, she decided morosely, depended on what she listened to—reason, or the strong sense of disappointment making her miserable. Oh, gosh. Had she misread the silent message in his eyes? Did she know what she really wanted?

Her gaze swung once more to Dominic as he bent, attending to Brutus. *She* might be ambivalent, but her eyes had no such doubts. Under lowered lashes, they had followed his movements as he'd chopped more wood, spoke to his dog, cleaned his impressive catch and generally kept himself occupied. Which had left her with little to do but sip more wine, savor the unfamiliar feeling of being cared for and deal with the slow burn going on in her mind.

She watched as Dominic stood and moved off on yet another task. Blair sighed, pulling her gaze away. Automatically, she checked the progress of the fire, shifted her legs to a more comfortable position and leaned back, lifting her face to the night sky. By now darkness had truly descended, and hundreds of stars formed a breathtaking canopy overhead.

Think peace and tranquility, Mackenzie. It's what you came for. Her breathing slowed, and gradually the beauty of the night caught her in its spell.

"You look like you're a million miles away."

Blair jumped, startled, as Dominic loomed up in the fire-light. With the added dimensions of his down-filled jacket, he looked as impressive as one of the surrounding mountains. Her heartbeat raced as she raised her eyes to his face. "Good grief. You've shaved!" she gasped.

Dominic's fingers stroked the clean lines of his jaw. "As promised." He grinned. "Tell me, was that a good 'good grief' or an exclamation of pure horror?"

Was he kidding? Dominic bearded was beautiful. Dominic *shaved* was nothing short of sensational. Reflections from the leaping flames cast shadows over the now visible contours of his face, masking his eyes while highlighting his strong, straight nose, prominent cheekbones, the set determination of his mobile mouth.

Blair felt her mouth go dry in a silence that stretched too long. "You'll probably pass in the dark," she finally teased, casting lightness into her voice. "At least there's no longer any doubt in my mind."

"Thanks a lot," he said. "Doubt about what? Although I may be sorry I asked."

She raised her eyes from the formidable line of his "weak" jaw. "You could be, so I'll take the coward's way out by refusing to answer. How's Brutus doing?" she asked, changing the subject.

"Logy and looking for sympathy, but otherwise fair. I need to talk to you about that, by the way. One of a number of things up for discussion tonight."

The sensual undertones were back in his voice, and Blair's stomach knotted in a renewed war of emotions. "Oh?" she responded, coming up blank with any form of challenge she cared to voice.

"Oh," he confirmed. "Besides which, I've brought you something tailor-made for the inner man . . . and woman." He gestured with his hands; she saw that he held their mugs.

"What makes me suspect it isn't coffee?" She hesitated, then curved her slim fingers around one of the handles.

"Brandy," he confirmed, dropping down beside her. He stretched out his long denim-clad legs with a casualness she could only envy, then leaned back to settle his shoulders against the hard face of the boulder. By accident or design, they now touched from shoulder to thigh. "Go ahead. Try some. It's almost as mellow as I am."

"Let's hope it's easier to swallow," she said dryly. The air had stirred with his descent. Blair caught the unmistakable scent of him . . . clean, evocative, distinct. Mixed with night wind and woodsmoke, it was a volatile combination.

"Mellowing, my crisp little chrysanthemum, is more closely connected to what I had planned for the night's entertainment. Unless—" his voice turned potently agreeable "—you had something else in mind . . ." His eyes glowed in the light of the fire.

"It's *your* mind I seriously question. White wine with dinner, beer, ice, a carton of special honey and now this. Your backpack must weigh a ton."

"Everything has its price." His sigh was deep enough to set tremors running along the ground. "Which, I suppose, is as good a lead-in as any to what I have to tell you."

About to sample the liqueur, Blair hesitated at the black tone in Dom's voice. Curious, she turned her head, surprised to find his mouth grim, eyes even more so. A sliver of foreboding touched her heart. "That sounds a little ominous."

"As far as you and I are concerned, it is."

Blair's head began to pound as a lesson learned early in life took hold. Be prepared for whatever comes. Her thoughts raced through a plethora of possibilities, but what was the absolute worst he could mention?

Married, her mind shot back.

No! *Not possible.* He'd said unequivocally he wasn't.

All right, then. Seriously involved.

She tightened in shock. Not only possible, but probable! What woman in her right mind would turn him down?

Hadn't she herself almost succumbed before caution prevailed? A weekend's harmless flirting. She'd said all along it couldn't be real. Tears stung her eyes as the ache in her clenched fingers brought her gaze down to her mug. Brandy, she thought grimly, was a damned good idea. She took a healthy swallow. It burned all the way down but helped numb the sense of utter loss ricocheting around in her stomach. She would *not* react. She set her teeth and kept silent, flashing him a look that should have sliced him in half.

Most of which Dom caught. "I know just how you feel," he said roughly. "I've spent the better part of the afternoon trying to figure some way I could get out of it, but I can't."

Get out of it? Fumes from the potent liqueur jammed her mental processes, and for a moment she was speechless. "Wait just a minute. What are you saying?"

"That I have to leave sometime tomorrow."

"And?"

"There's no way I can stay. I've a full surgery schedule slated Monday morning, and if I'm going to be back in time..." He shrugged in irritated resignation.

Blair waited for a long, tense moment. "You mean that's *it*?"

He looked at her, eyes now a little wary. "Not quite."

She braced herself. Here it comes.

"I'm afraid I'll have to leave Brutus behind... with you. His leg isn't strong enough yet to take the trip down." He turned to face her. "I'm sorry. I know it's a lot to ask—"

Blair waved a hand, cutting him off. "Is that *it*?" she insisted. "There's nothing else you have to tell me?"

"Isn't that enough?" he rumbled with full-throttled disgust.

She couldn't help it. She started to laugh. At him, although he didn't know it. But mostly at herself. Relief, pure and perfect, poured through her veins. She had thought she'd lost... something of immense importance.

"What is all this, Mackenzie?" Dom growled.

"What is what?" she asked innocently, draining the brandy. It...and life...were beautiful.

"Is all this sudden hilarity due to the fact I'm leaving or because I asked you to take care of the dog? Or both?"

"Oh, Dominic." She smiled tenderly at his scowling face. "Neither one, I assure you."

"Then I'm not sure I understand."

"Neither did I. But it's okay," she answered softly. "Not about your leaving," Blair added quickly. "I'm...not happy you must go. As for Brutus—" she rushed on before he could take advantage of her admission "—I'll do my best, although I'm not sure whether I can handle him properly or not."

"We'll work on that in the morning until you feel comfortable with it. You needn't worry. Not only does he love you, but he's been well trained."

"Now, why does neither factor in that last statement relieve my mind?"

He chuckled deep in his chest and leaned forward to throw another log on the fire. "Trust me."

She did...now, she thought. Her stomach still felt the aftershocks of her frightening assumption. She spoke before she lost courage. "Dom?" He turned his head to look back at her. "I'm sorry you have to leave tomorrow. For some reason I assumed you'd be here...longer." The word seemed inadequate but was the only one she could think of that wouldn't be incriminating.

Dominic's smile faded, and he straightened, maneuvering his large body away from the fire to face her. "No more sorry than I. There's still too much left unsaid, undone, between us, Blair." He ran a frustrated hand through his thick shock of dark hair. "Dammit. Normally, my Mondays are free."

"So are mine," she offered impulsively.

"I'll remember that, so plan to spend a lot of them together." His face registered a wealth of chagrin. "I picked a hell of a time to catch up on some minor procedures, didn't I? What I wouldn't give right now for a handy treeside telephone to cancel them all out."

She'd give a lot herself. "A little harder to do than getting rid of a beard," she agreed, echoing in full the depths of his regret.

Though his face was in shadow, his eyes gleamed. "If memory serves, there's a bit of unfinished business connected to that." He settled his hands on her shoulders with infinite purpose. "Remember?"

As if branded on her forehead. Blair brushed her fingers along his clean-shaven cheek. "I like you this way," she offered, her voice soft.

He eased her more deeply into his arms. "I like me this way, too. Close enough to hold you, feel your body against mine, to breathe in the beauty of your fragrance. You're lovely, Blair. Inside and out."

"You can't really know that," she murmured above the thud of her heart.

"Ah, but I do. Look at me."

She raised her eyes from the intriguing lines of his mouth. "What do you see?"

"Laugh lines," she teased him, breathless. Then raised her other hand to his face, holding him still as she considered. "Strength, perceptiveness, integrity."

"You can't really know that," he denied, using her own argument against her.

"Wrong, Mr. Know-it-all," she denied in a throaty whisper. "The creases are right here." She traced them with gentle fingers, picking up the strong pulse beat in his temples.

"I see you in the same way, Blair. In your lips, in your face, in your eyes. In what you say, how you move."

His words, his breath, the soft texture of his mouth, brushed softly against her lips, and she couldn't stand it. Her tongue came out to taste him.

The electrifying contact cost Dominic his control. One of them moaned as his mouth came down beautifully on hers. Desperation brought them to their knees, his huge hands arching her small body upward into the hard haven of his arms. "Take me in," he whispered hoarsely against her lips, and he kissed her.

She drew his questing tongue deep, deep into the warm inner recesses of her mouth. He tasted of brandy, of male need so strong it made her tremble. And she answered with an equal demand, hands linked behind his bold head, as her body responded, ripening to the heat, the thrusting tension in his loins.

In the periphery of her mind, she felt the discomfort of loose gravel biting into her knees, but his hands had moved from the rounded softness of her hips, up under her thick jacket, finding the way inside her shirt. Roughened fingers whispered against silken skin to release her bra. Her small breasts burst free, nipples ripe and eager for him. And as his hands closed over her sensitized, swollen flesh, she moaned, her own loins long since moist and warm and wanting. "Dominic, please," she pleaded brokenly, wondering if he could hear her cry over the thunder of their heartbeats.

"Ah, Blair, so special, so perfect," he answered, his voice a harsh, muffled sound as he buried his lips in the base of her throat. "I ache for the taste of you, the feel of you, in my mouth, on my body—everywhere, Blair. Everywhere."

He moved his hands to fumble for the opening of her jacket, and she dropped her arms from his shoulders to help him not only with hers but with his, needing as much as he did the contact of bare skin against bare skin. She opened her eyes, reaching for snaps... and froze, a garbled sound caught in her throat.

Three feet away, Brutus stared back with wide doggie eyes, panting, tongue lolling and ears cocked forward with avid interest.

"Dominic, stop!" She snatched the front of her jacket out of his grasp. Her face burned with embarrassment and was as red, she was sure, as the campfire.

"What?" Disoriented, Dominic was slow to react. "Blair, what are you saying?" He dug his fingers into her shoulders, his eyes flaring with remnants of passion.

"I can't," she wailed, burying her hot face into his broad chest. "I just can't."

"Can't...?" He bit back a curse as his hands moved to frame her head, forcing her to look up at him. "What happened?" he demanded. "Dammit, Blair. You were *with* me. What changed your mind?"

His eyes, she saw, were stormy gray and growing dangerous, and she squared her jaw. She was more than a little upset herself, come to think of it. "I don't know what *your* habits are, but I won't be watched!"

"*Watched?* What in hell are you talking about?"

"*Him,*" she said with royal outrage, and pointed.

Gravel spurted as Dom got to his feet in time to see his personal version of man's best friend sit back on his haunches and flash them a toothy grin. "*Woof!*" Brutus said eagerly.

Oh, for Pete's sake, Blair thought as her anger drained. She let her body sag to her heels as she watched the tension drain from Dominic's broad back. Her eyes went to his face as he slowly turned, features wry, mouth rueful. "The him, I take it, refers to this four-footed voyeur."

"Who else?" she said, and sighed in resignation.

"For a second there, I wasn't entirely sure. My apologies, sweetheart. For someone with his intelligence, at times he can be downright dim-witted. Let me bed him down for the night, then I'll be right back."

"Will he *stay*?"

Dominic's mouth firmed. "He'll stay, all right. The question is, will you?"

Blair nodded. "Someone has to keep an eye on the fire," she said, hedging.

"You won't let it die completely before I get back, will you?"

In a voice so low and intense, the loaded question almost made her laugh. Considering the ache in her unbound breasts and the fierce frustration elsewhere, she knew there wasn't a snowball's chance in Haiti that could happen. He had to know that, had to be hurting nearly as much.

"Blair?" he said expectantly, taking a step forward.

She breathed deeply, looked at him and shook her head.

His smile made her melt inside as he turned, snapped his fingers impatiently at the dog and strode into the darkness.

Blair remained as she was, crossing her arms as if to guard the inner blaze, eyes fixed on the spot where Dominic had disappeared, her mind in limbo as she waited.

And he was back suddenly, dousing the fire, lifting her to her feet and holding her fast as she momentarily stumbled.

"What are you doing?" Blair whispered, confused.

"As of right now, this camp is shut down for the night."

"But it's early—"

"Not for what I have in mind."

A wave of weakness washed straight to her knees. "Where are we going?" she said, gasping as his big hands caught her close.

"To find a softer bed. I don't know about you, but gravel biting into my backside cuts down on my concentration."

She was swept up into his arms, any protest she might have made muffled by his mouth on hers, warm and demanding.

"This is crazy," she said when she could, her voice hazed with the wild, sweet singing in her bloodstream.

"And inevitable from the first moment I saw you." His lips traced warmth, sensation, over her eyelids, her temples, the corners of her mouth. "Your place or mine?" he murmured gruffly.

His place was out in the open, nothing but a sleeping bag. She wanted walls to close them in, wrap them in the private security of their own world. "Mine," she answered in soft surrender, and slowly releasing his breath, Dominic took several strides forward to lower her in front of her tent flap.

Not certain she could stand, Blair clung to his arm, facing his towering form, which was barely discernible against the star-studded sky. Oh, gosh. This wasn't wise, wasn't rational. She wasn't sure she was ready. "Dominic," she began in a tremulous voice.

"Cold feet?" he guessed, melting her protest with the heat of his mouth. "I promise you I'll have them warm in no time at all."

The low, thrumming vow uttered against her lips dissolved the last shred of her resistance. With Dominic guiding her actions, she bent low, entering the inky darkness of the tent, feeling the air stir as if in anticipation. She couldn't see, only heard the rustle of clothing removed, and then his hands found her, came around, enfolding her into the encompassing strength of his body as his weight bore them down to the soft padding of her sleeping bag.

With her hands she found his waist above his jeans, the slick texture of his bare back, and she slid her fingertips upward, breathless in the wonder of exploration, pleasure seeping in through all her senses.

His mouth was everywhere, in her hair, on her forehead, on the closed lids of her eyes. "Blair," he groaned, "my small, sweet treasure. It seems I've waited a lifetime for this."

"You haven't known me that long," she murmured hazily, abstracted by his scent, his soft hair against her lips as his tongue traced the line of her throat.

"I knew you were out there somewhere. I just had to find you." His hands moved, releasing the buttons of her shirt to warm the swollen mounds of her breasts. Supple fingers whispered across her nipples, paused, tormented, and she moaned, wanting the pull of his mouth to ease their aching fullness. "Dom, oh, Dom," she begged, arching against his palms.

He lowered his head and drew each thrusting peak in turn into the inner heat of his mouth, tongue tasting, stroking, suckling, sending streams of liquid languor throughout her lower body. Inner tremors like small potent explosions seared straight through her as his hands moved, slid to the waistband of her jeans to free the fastenings. Her stomach muscles contracted as purposeful fingers dipped, brushing downward toward the moist heat of her thighs. And then, as his mouth covered hers, he found her and she cried out as he stroked deep into the sanctuary of her hidden essence. Her fingernails dug into his skin as his tongue thrust in equal penetration, in synchronizing forays.

Her mind spun as pressure built, then climbed higher, until she shimmered apart...a torrential release she'd never fully experienced.

Before her cries faded, he gathered her against the massive contours of his body, his voice a husky croon in her ear, "Blair, you're so beautiful, you take my breath away." His fingers trembled against her breast. "Let me share it, my own. Bury myself in your softness. I have to be a part of you."

As she needed to be his, if only for tonight. Tomorrow he would be gone, leaving her to handle the repercussions, but at the moment she didn't care. "Yes," she breathed, on fire, wanting his full, throbbing masculinity to sear them together in ultimate fusion. "My boots," Blair added frantically. "Let me take off—"

A hard, brief kiss cut off her words. "Let me," he commanded, his gruffness belied by the shakiness of his hands as he searched in the dark for her lacings.

Blair shifted, reaching for the thongs on her other foot, not willing to wait. In her haste she was clumsy, and from a muffled oath she knew Dominic's impatience matched her own. At last, her small feet were free, and as his hands found her jeans, she lifted her hips so he could slide both them and the brief wisp of her panties down the silken length of her legs. Cold air hit her and she shivered, missing his warmth, needing the blanketing of his massive body in, over, around her.

The muted thud of his shoes thrown to one side, the snick of snaps, the sound of first a zipper and then the glide of denim down hair-roughened legs had her heart turning over in her breast. Hurry, she urged him silently.

Before her mind had finished forming the plea, he was there, sliding her shirt, then her bra, off her shoulders and down her arms. Only he was real...hard and warm, bare and vital, gathering the soft, eager curves of her body into the long, hungry length of him as his mouth traced heated patterns over her face. "You feel so good." His mouth sought the fullness of her lips. "I'll never get enough of you, the taste of you...your mouth..." He sampled her singular delectability with his tongue. "The perfection of your breasts..." Her hands fell to his shoulders as his mouth closed over each mound in scalding assault. "Your sweet-scented skin."

"Dom, *please*," she almost sobbed, not sure whether it was protest or plea. She pressed her hands against his head, urging him upward, finding his mouth with hers. His touch was everywhere, stroking, conquering, reducing her to a vessel of twisting need. She moved her hands in frenzied urgency over the vibrant flowing muscles of his broad back, his sides, to the fine sheen of hair covering his powerful thighs.

His harsh intake of breath as she touched him shuddered through his whole body. "I need you, Blair. Now. Tomorrow. Forever."

"Oh, Dominic..." A breath of hope, of expectancy, fractured her voice.

"We'll take it slow and easy." With infinite gentleness, he eased himself slowly against the restriction of her thighs. And she opened to him, arms, legs, urging him closer. Then, unbelievably, she felt him stiffen in resistance, his breath a ragged sound in his throat.

"Blair, no. Wait."

The agonized words stabbed her straight in the heart. What was wrong?

"Honey," he gasped against her mouth, "is this safe? I'm...not prepared. I can't protect you."

"I'm fine," she murmured, thankful beyond measure that she was. "It's all right."

She was so touched by his concern, she had to speak above the tears forming in her heart. Oh, Mackenzie, her soul cried out, you could easily love this man. She reached up with trembling fingers to stroke the slightly roughened texture of his newly shaven jawline. "Thank you for asking, Dominic," she whispered.

His sigh was earthshaking as he captured her fingers, kissed her palm.

His hands moved to the sweet roundness of her buttocks as his mouth hovered above hers. "You are...beautiful, love," he murmured, and as his tongue entered her willing lips, she rose to meet him, taking him far into the molten reaches of her femininity.

Wave upon wave of sensation shot through her as he took her deeper, bringing her to the edge of ultimate agony until, head writhing, she burst apart, her cries spilling out in the dark enclosure.

A moment later his harsh cry joined hers amid a fire storm of explosive release. Heart, soul, body, they were bound together, and Blair clung to him, feeling his mouth buried in the damp tendrils of her hair, hearing the whisper of words she couldn't distinguish, yet reading their meaning through her pores. The heady scent of their passion infused her senses as tears of repletion formed in her eyes. Never in her brief experience had she known such physical ecstasy. It left her mind reeling.

Slowly, she ran her hands up his sweat-slicked back, reveling in the evidence of his cataclysmic emotions—the thud of his heart against her breasts, the sheen of perspiration still fusing their bodies in fulfillment. She loved the feel of him, the carefully controlled weight of him, and couldn't care less if she never moved.

But long before she was ready, he shifted, edging himself to his hands and knees, and she murmured a protest as cool air flowed over her sensitized skin.

"Are you okay, my own?" he asked.

His husky concern made her smile. "I'm fine," she assured him softly. Actually, she felt wonderful, beyond words in a few oh-so-right places.

"I didn't hurt you, did I? I'm not too heavy...?"

"You didn't, and you're not. You're just right."

"Oh, Blair," he murmured, "so are you." His mouth touched hers gently, but with a stroke of deep-rooted possession. "You're mine, my love, as I'm now yours in every sense of the word."

"Mmm," she answered noncommittally. For the moment it was true, Blair thought, closing her mind to concerns over tomorrow's reality. Right now, this man, this time, this night, were hers to savor.

Dom's low voice broke into her musings. "Sweetheart, you can't be comfortable. I hate to mention the mundane, but my backside is beginning to freeze."

In the pitch darkness she picked up the lazy humor in his tones. His eyes, she knew, would be filled with his special brand of amusement, and she smiled. With a heady feeling of freedom, she moved her hands to check. "Why, 'pon my soul, sir, so it is!"

"Imp." Dom dropped a kiss somewhere in the vicinity of her forehead, eased back, then rolled away.

Cold air swept over her body, and as Blair yelped, Dominic laughed, found an end of her sleeping bag and tucked it in around her shoulders. "Hang on. I'll be right back."

"What, if I dare ask, are you doing?"

"Ensuring us a long and comfortable night. Reinforcements coming right up."

She caught a glimpse of his quick-moving frame silhouetted against the star-bright sky before her tent flap dropped down, bringing a billow of even colder air into the enclosure. Blair shivered and burrowed into the welcome warmth of her covering.

Within seconds he was back, attaching his sleeping bag to hers, gathering her small body back into his arms, warming his chilled flesh with her heat. She gave willingly, entangling her legs in his as she rubbed her hands over the broad reaches of his back.

"That feels good," he groaned. "It's damned cold out there."

"Serves you right for barreling out of here buck naked."

"Why put something on to take it right back off again?" he asked with smug male reason.

"I'm a little surprised you didn't bring the brandy as well."

His hands paused on her rib cage. "Do you want some?"

"No," she whispered, vividly aware of the impossibly delicious things going on under the covers. "I believe I have everything I need right here."

With a growl, Dominic made sure she did.

Eleven

There was, Blair decided drowsily, something both sinfully delicious and simply scary about waking at dawn in Dominic Masters's arms. On the one hand, it could lead to a most interesting morning. On the other, it promised complex and complicated problems. When she allowed herself to think about it, she realized she was already in over her head.

Reluctant to acknowledge the first rays of sunshine poking their way persistently through the seams of her tent, she closed her eyes, preferring to shelve the questions, wise or otherwise, that she'd have to face. For a few precious moments, she lay still, breathing in the familiar ambience, the wonderful warmth curling around her as she nestled in Dominic's lax embrace.

Operative word: *lax*.

She knew better.

Each time she'd unconsciously shifted during the night, she'd been hauled back into his arms, the curve of his shoulder her pillow, his big, beautiful body her shelter, his hand on her breast her anchor. Even in sleep, Dominic was a persevering, possessive man. Those traits loomed large in her mind as a fascinating, worrisome factor.

With a sigh, she stretched her leg, needing to flex her sore knee, and felt Dominic's body quicken.

"So you *are* awake," he rumbled close to her ear. "I wondered."

Blair let him turn her to face him, angling her slender limbs away from his potentially dangerous thighs as she met the quizzical warmth in his eyes. "Good morning," she said demurely. He looked sleep-tousled, yet alert, and his smile increased as he stroked the clinging tendrils of her mahogany curls from the side of her face.

"I believe it has all the earmarks. I surely do," he murmured, zeroing in on her mouth. He moved his hands in a slow tactile exploration that made her catch her breath. "How are you feeling, my love?"

Pleasurably tender here and there, but she wasn't about to complain. "Perfect," she managed to whisper as the beginnings of another beard grazed her cheek. If she were one of his fuzzy, four-footed friends, she'd probably purr. Slanting him a mischievous look, she lazily traced the line of his lower lip with her finger. "How about you? No regrets?"

Although he chuckled, his eyes were beginning to look smoky and intent, and her face grew warm as tension rose between them.

She was uncomfortably sure that more than his lovemaking had impressed itself on her heart as he brushed his lips against hers and whispered, "I have no regrets. And no doubts."

"Neither," she murmured, "do I. Not about this."

Blair placed her small hand on his chest, on the smooth surface covering the strong beat of his heart, hoping neither her tone of voice nor the slight slip of her tongue betrayed the instinctive uneasiness she felt over the future of their relationship.

She'd forgotten the depth of his perceptiveness. Dominic levered himself up on an elbow, pinning her with not only the thoughtful focus of his gaze but a bronzed hair-roughened arm as well. "Why do I have the feeling there's doubt dangling from the end of that statement?"

Mentally squirming, having hemmed herself in, Blair broke contact with his eyes. Her glance had skimmed down past his waist before she realized where it had strayed. With a silent groan, she raised her lashes, marshalling words like small weapons in a dismally supplied arsenal. "Probably because there is," she answered reluctantly.

"About where this will lead? There's no question whatsoever in *my* mind."

His tone held singular purpose, and Blair sighed. She could almost see the arguments forming in his mind. But she wasn't exactly taking a stand from a position of strength, bare as the day she was born and flat on her back with him poised over her. Why hadn't she waited until she was garrisoned in some clothes and fortified with her third cup of coffee? "Look, couldn't we discuss this somewhere else?"

A shamelessly sexy gleam grew in his eyes. "Another time, another place," he agreed softly. "Which leaves us with the here and now." His arms tightened and her soul quivered as a powerful thigh slid over her lower body, pressing its considerable advantage into the soft warmth it found. "Doesn't it, my love?"

"Oh, Dominic," she whispered as a river of heat flooded her loins. "Yes!"

It was the last coherent thing she said for over an hour.

One might argue, Blair thought as she ran her hand through her short crop of curls, that this was also not the time or the place for the type of discussion she had in mind. But packed and ready to leave or not, Dominic had to be put straight in his thinking before he set one foot out of the campsite.

For hours, his whole demeanor had implied he'd won his battle of persistent pursuit. But as far as she was concerned, one night of mutual surrender did not mean peace had been signed in their personal war of wills.

Reality—who and what she was—waited in Edmonds, and she was not about to let him go off assuming that once she got home, they'd pick up where they left off—in other words, intrinsically entwined.

It couldn't possibly work that way. Not with so many basic differences between them.

"You're sure I've left enough food?"

Dom's question cut short her mental monologue. "Good grief, yes. I could feed an army."

He laughed as he tightened the last strap on his pack and turned to face her. "You might think you're doing just that. Brutus eats enough for a platoon."

It was the least of her worries. "I'll manage." Blair stuffed her hands in her jeans pockets, watching the play of light on Dominic's huge frame. Shoulders and chest swelled the thin fabric of his blue T-shirt. Emblazoned across the front in bold black letters was the name of his boat, *The Cat's Meow*. The same could be said of him, she thought with a sigh. The powerful contours of his hips, thighs and legs challenged the seams of his well-worn jeans. Even his hiking boots looked beautiful to her, Blair mused in self-mockery. In an incredibly short time, this huge man had made enormous inroads on her perspective. It was a good thing he was leaving. Alone, she'd be able to get her priorities back on track. For some reason, she frowned, and dropped her gaze to the ground.

"Sweetheart, are you sure you feel confident about handling him?"

"Of course." After a very late breakfast, under Dominic's tutelage, she'd changed Brutus's dressing, stored the necessary medical supplies in her tent, and then worked with the affable animal until everyone concerned was satisfied with command and obedience. "We'll be okay."

"Then what's bothering you?" Dom's voice became low and vibrant as he took a step closer.

"How soon do you have to leave?"

He gave her a long look, then glanced at his watch. "About fifteen minutes. I don't want to cut it too close."

"Don't take any risks, Dom." Her heart tripped at the thought.

"Don't worry, darlin'. I'll be back down at my car well before dark." It was his turn to frown. "I might give you the same warning. Brutus will be able to travel by tomorrow or the next day, but don't try to head down until that knee of yours feels up to it. Do you hear me? And take your sweet time when you do."

"Orders again, Masters?" Blair squared her shoulders just as his hands closed over them, his determination rampant in every finger.

"In this case, yes." His smile was off kilter, but there was steel underneath. "Do you mind?"

It was an opening she had to use. "As a matter of fact, I do. I'm quite able to draw conclusions and make my own decisions, which is something you seem to have a hard time accepting."

"Hey, wait a minute. I said that for your own—"

"Good? I've heard *that* before!"

The strength of her resentment caught him by surprise. "I see," he said evenly. Then, with a gentle hand, he tilted her chin so she was forced to meet his eyes. "I've had a feeling for the past hour or so that something was simmering below the surface. Tell me what's really bothering you, Blair."

She hesitated. He towered over her. The breadth of his body combined with his hands sending silent messages to her heart made her feel smaller than she'd ever felt, and nearly overwhelmed. She firmed her jaw. Darn it, she had more grit than this! "The truth?"

Dominic's clear gray eyes softened. "Always."

"You won't like it," she warned him.

That made him smile. "Try me."

"It's about your expectations," she plunged in before she could change her mind.

"What about my...expectations?" He began to move his thumbs back and forth, sliding them over the soft fabric of her shirt as if in search of her soft curves.

"I want you to think about them while you're gone," she said over the constriction building in her throat.

"I don't stand a chance of thinking about anything else, darlin'. I guarantee it. Which means a lot of cold showers."

Oh, help. He wasn't getting the point at all. "You haven't even heard what I'm trying to say. Quit jumping to conclusions."

"So talk." His grin became wider. "I'm listening."

That low, sexy murmur told her his mind was straying farther into dangerous channels, and she had to fight off the wave of sensual weakness flooding her system. She and Dominic might be highly compatible in this one area, but in every other they weren't even close. "Please. This has happened too fast. I'm—"

"Having second thoughts?"

"Shouldn't I be? This is crazy, Dom. We have nothing in common."

His incredulous rumble rose in the air. *"Nothing?"*

"Well, almost nothing," she conceded. "Think about it." Heaven knew *she* was trying. "You love animals; I don't. Cats make me sneeze, and boats turn me green."

"Honey, those are peripherals. I promise you, I'll leave at work anything connected with it."

"But *I* don't." Her voice grew a little desperate as he lowered his head to brush his lips against her temple in sweet assault. "That's what's so scary. You said yourself you were indifferent to art, and galleries in particular. It's a repudiation of everything I live for." Her voice dropped to a whisper. "It's...it's not going to work."

"You forgot to mention I'm an only child," Dom murmured helpfully as his mouth trailed along the line of her jaw.

"What?" Oh. Oh, yes. "That...that, too," Blair managed, dimly aware of a warning in the back of her mind. Hadn't she had it up to here with that particular breed?

"Wipe one objection off your list, my love," he whispered against the pulse point of her throat. "Peg's an absolute marvel."

Blair's emotional level plunged to her toes. Dom's unfortunate choice of words was an echo of her ex-husband's defense of *his* mother. What did she really know about this man—what he thought, how he acted—other than what he'd let her see? She needed the chance to think.

She slipped free of his embrace and made herself step back, ignoring the look in his eyes. "It's...time for you to leave."

Dominic's mouth set. "What happened?"

"Nothing." She looked away. *"Don't!"* she pleaded as he took a step forward. "It's just that it's getting late. You have to go." Her voice was a little unsteady, but she managed a smile.

"Unfortunately, I have no choice along those lines." He swore, then ran his strong fingers through the unruly wealth of his hair. "I'd give anything to stay. You know that." His eyes fairly sparked with emotion. "Listen to me, sweetheart," he urged her roughly, sidestepping her warning and closing his hands over her shoulders. His smile resurfaced, rueful but ripe with understanding. "As much as it pains me to admit it, I guess you have the right to wonder whether I'm—or this is—real. Believe me when I say that who and what I am has been out in the open for you to see. No closet cravings, no evil habits or hidden vices." His smile surfaced as chagrin filled her eyes. "Aside from the ones you've accused me of, that is. And being the adaptable man I am, I'm sure we'll find a way to surmount those . . . together. I'm *not* letting you get away."

Bemused at the uncanny way he had of reading her mind, Blair stammered, "But . . ."

"As for having nothing in common, my dear," he persisted, "look around you. Where did we meet? Don't we share a passion for the outdoors? You've made friends with Brutus, and my brand of humor meshes with yours as beautifully as our bodies. That's more than enough basis for a lasting love affair."

His soft words, the heat of his hands burning through her thin shirt, made her mind spin.

"As for the differences—" He brushed her brow with his lips as his voice grew husky. "Mmm . . . I positively adore your differences."

As she did his. Oh, Dominic, her heart cried as his mouth lowered on hers, as his hard, masculine arms gathered her into the sweet sanctuary of his large body. And all her cautiousness, her careful arguments, fractured, leaving but one thought: It was the last time he'd hold her for who knew how many days. Blair surrendered herself to the moment . . . and to him

"I have to go," he whispered against her lips.

"I know."

"Call me as soon as you get home, promise?"

"Yes."

"Goodbye, my love."

"Goodbye. Take care." But neither moved until, with a muffled curse, Dominic forced himself away, turned and, with grim determination hitched his pack up onto his back. His eyes roved over her face in a long, lingering look, then angled off to her side. "Brutus, stay. Guard," he said sternly, then again met her gaze. "Make it back soon, or I'm liable to wring your lovely neck.'' Then he scowled and strode away.

She caught a quick movement out of the corner of her eye and whipped her head around. "No! Brutus, stay!" She lunged for the anxious dog. Blair wrapped her arms around his thick shoulders, burying her fists in his fur. "It's all right," she said soothingly, wishing she believed it herself, and as he obeyed, she raised her head to stare through a mist of tears at the wall of undergrowth beyond which Dominic had disappeared.

A keening whimper made her tighten her hold as she met Brutus's sad eyes. "You cry," she warned him darkly, blinking hard, "and I'll never speak to you again!" She struggled to her feet, keeping one hand on his collar. "Come on, you overgrown baby. We can live without him for a couple of days."

As she tugged him along, ignoring the added stress on her knee, she hoped the dog had more faith in her words than she did. The campsite already rang with loneliness.

After several sun-drenched, miserable days and sleepless nights, Blair had done enough soul-searching to last her a lifetime. Checking the status of Brutus's wound soon after dawn on the third day, she made the decision to leave. Within an hour, she'd struck her tent and packed, adrenaline flowing through her veins. Her knee be damned; she was heading for home. And Dom.

Love—yes, darn it, *love*—thrives on challenges, on compromise, she thought, casting one last, nostalgic glance around the pristine meadow. Opposites attract after all. And at the moment she was *burning* with attraction!

Whistling an excited Brutus into line, Blair turned and plunged through the underbrush, her step not light, but sure.

Her morning euphoria gradually wilted under the less-than-expeditious trip downtrail, the discovery of a flat tire once she reached her car, then Brutus's hot doggy breath steaming all over her neck from the back seat as she fought the traffic to her cutoff. But as she crested the hill at the south end of town, her heart raced at the sight of the city's lights. She caught a glimpse of a huge ferry, lit like a welcome-home party, out on the Sound and grinned. It, like she, was entering a familiar harbor.

Energy surged through her bloodstream. Challenging the speed limit, she shot down the slope of the avenue.

Despite the early start, dusk had fallen before she was able to maneuver her small station wagon into the parking space behind the sprawling structure that held her home and business. As she turned off the ignition, Blair tried to suppress her excitement. Dominic's telephone number burned into her side through a zippered pocket. First things first, Mackenzie. There was a hundred and fifty pounds of puppy in need of a walk after hours of confinement, plus her gear to unload. *Then* she could give in to the temptation to call Dominic. What would he say? Heat flooded her lower abdomen as she remembered the sound and texture of his sexy rumble, and she all but fell out of the car in her hurry.

With a woof of excitement, Brutus followed her out like a moving mountain of fur and disappeared, blending into the darkness. But as she hauled her backpack up the narrow wooden stairs that led to her second-floor apartment, he pressed his cold, wet nose into her thigh. Either he'd been in a hurry, or he was nervous about being left behind. "It's okay, you big lug. Quit worrying. This is the end of the line," Blair assured him as she unlocked her door.

A stream of stale air greeted her as she stepped into her compact kitchen and snapped on the light. She laughed as the dog rushed past her, sniffed his way around the gleaming tile floor and vanished down the hallway. "Make yourself at home," she called dryly, hoping nothing breakable stood in the path of his tail.

Though she heard nothing crash, she dropped her pack next to one of the white wicker chairs by her tiny breakfast table and followed the curious animal's trail past her minuscule bathroom into the living room, trying to assess her apartment not through her own eyes but through Dominic's... not if but *when* he saw it. The thought gave her the shivers.

The building had once contained a flourishing florist/ nursery and the solid second floor had been nothing more than an L-shaped storage loft for hundreds of planting pots and bags of fertilizer and potting mix. With more ingenuity than money, Blair, with her partners' help, turned the short part of that L into a slightly confined but well-loved home. A shoulder-high wall separated the living area from her bedroom, which was graced with a half wall of windows. She had a spectacular view of the Sound and the snow-capped Olympic Mountains. In late afternoon, when sunshine washed past clouds, her decor of cream, gold, soft olive and mellow browns warmed not only her heart but her senses. Feeling somewhat reassured, she smiled.

A small sound caught her attention, and Blair moved forward to find Brutus ensconced in the middle of her bed. "Off, you presumptuous brute," she scolded him. "No one sleeps in there but me."

Her pulse quickened. Would that hold true once she called Dominic? The thought of him, of his huge, beautiful body, of their passionate joining amid her sheets, filled her inner vision, robbing her of breath. She ached with the need to reach him. Now.

Blair spun and sped for the phone in her kitchen, Brutus matching her stride for stride. Before she could dial, a deep-throated growl made her pause. She glanced quickly at the dog, and her gaze flew to the second door in her kitchen.

Beyond lay the long arm of the second-floor L. It held her balcony studio, a makeshift storage area and a wide set of stairs leading down to the gallery, from which, she realized, came the faint murmur of voices.

More puzzled than anything else, she ordered Brutus to be quiet as she stepped forward, slid back the lock and opened the door.

Not only light but the buzz of rather strident conversation rose from the gallery floor, out of which Blair could distinguish the voices of her partners. She'd timed her return just right, she thought. Something was brewing.

A rush of affection filled her heart. It was good to be back. "It's okay, boy. Relax." With an added order that he stay put, she closed the door behind her. She'd better prepare them for the black baby elephant first, she realized, mouth curved in amusement.

It was the last light-headed thought she had for some time.

Twelve

———

Thus man shall rise or fall through the printed word," Blair said with a groan less than an hour later. "And I think I just bit the dust."

Great Caesar's Ghost, a printing error. She still couldn't believe it! Every last one of the gallery's carefully crafted brochures was winging its way in a hundred different directions, via the U.S. mail, emblazoned with the wrong opening date. They now had less than three weeks, instead of well over two months, in which to mount their major fall show.

No wonder panic had reerupted the minute she'd shown her unsuspecting face. And while blame had been shouldered by each of her apologetic partners before they'd left, Blair still felt dazed with the self-reproach of twenty-twenty hindsight. She should have been *here*, not up in the mountains, when the final proofs had come in.

Blame and guilt were nonproductive, darn it. She needed to act, not wallow in wimpy hand wringing. With a frown, she stepped away from the glass-fronted counter against which she'd been leaning. Could she put it together in time and complete her own projects as well?

What choice did she have?

Her stride grew firm as she headed for her office. No bigger than a closet, it was the nerve center of the cooperative. More important, it held her concise notes.

But as she flicked on the light, her gaze fastened first on the phone, and she stopped short. Ohmigosh...Dominic! Belatedly she realized the task she faced meant putting her personal life—*him*—on hold until she'd salvaged the show. Her mind spun as the thought tore at her heart. Then slowly she shook her head. She had a professional crisis on her hands. He'd either understand...or he wouldn't.

Her teeth sank into her lip as Blair sat at her desk and reached for a pad and pencil, forcing herself to concentrate. Where to begin?

Consignees, though most of them were still following the summer art-fair circuit.

Maggie Cappelini...ASAP. Blair reached for the phone, her mind beginning to click with precision. Maggie was the only one Blair knew who had artistic contacts that stretched over half the state. Blair figured with any luck, Maggie could also supply the names of a few high-caliber artists who might leap at the chance to be represented in an awkwardly early but well-publicized show. Blair's optimism began to resurface as she dialed.

"My dear child!" Over the phone, the older woman's energetic voice flowed with warmth. "What a lovely surprise. For a moment I thought it might be my son, but this is *much* more fun. It's been ages. How are you?"

Blair leaned back against the firm padding of her chair. "In the soup," she admitted honestly. "But if you're busy or expecting another call..."

"Neither, actually," the older woman said, laughing. "I'm sitting here in my usual evening dishabille, catching up on my reading, until I hear Doc come in. The poor boy's been up to his neck in patients every night this week."

Blair made a face. So the workaholic offspring was at it again. She was fond of Maggie, who was silver haired and endowed with the gift of poise. Maggie's intelligent blue eyes reflected an inexhaustible zest for her career, the arts and her son... not necessarily in that order. The latter... well! Considering her own close family ties and what she'd seen lacking between Greg and Bea, Blair didn't have much respect for a man who had so little time for his mother. Maggie had once mentioned that they didn't interfere in each other's life, but Blair had the impression he carried it to extremes. But she knew it was none of her business. "Nevertheless, I promise not to take more than a minute of your time," Blair said.

Maggie laughed. "Aside from buckets of unwanted advice, at *my* age time is the only interesting thing I have to offer. Now, what's this about soup? Knowing you, it's business rather than personal."

Blair smiled, remembering Maggie's occasional comment over what had been—until now—her rather sterile love life. A faint flush warmed her face as she answered, "Well, this happens to be strictly business."

"How disappointing," the older woman said with a sigh. "Ah, well. Let's see. It can't be a problem with the lease; I made sure of that. So it's something else. Fire away, my dear."

Wasting no words, Blair explained. Fifteen minutes later she had a list of names and a sense of buoyancy. "Terrific! This should go a long way in saving our skins."

"Nonsense," Maggie said. "There's no guarantee on any of them. All I've done is saddle you with a lot of legwork." She chuckled, then changed subjects. "That reminds me. When I dropped by the other day, they told me you'd gone hiking. Considering what you're facing the next three weeks, I hope you got more rest than exercise."

Without any warning, Dominic's face, warm and vital, rose in Blair's mind, and she laughed, unaware that her voice had grown husky. "Rest," she said softly, "isn't quite the word I would use, my friend."

There was a startled silence on the other end of the phone. "Unless my intuition's gone wacky, I'd swear I hear a male in there somewhere."

Blair's smile increased as she gave in to impulse. "As a matter of fact, you do."

"Good heavens, I can't believe it. Is it...that is... Are you saying it's serious?"

Having meant only to hint, Blair was both surprised and amused. She'd never heard Maggie that...vehement before. "Let's just say I'm *very* taken," she answered with belated caution.

"So that's that." There was a split second of silence. "Well." Maggie's voice took on a drawling note. "For your sake, Blair, I hope that whoever he is, he's perfect for you."

"Not quite accurate, but close enough!"

Which made them both laugh as they said good-night.

Minutes later, Blair stood under the welcome spray of a hot shower, her mind still racing with the challenges she faced.

Not the least of which was Dom, she mused as she toweled dry and slipped into a thin nightgown. The magic in and out of the mountains was one thing; reality another. Would he admire the gallery even a tiny bit? Approve of her judgment? Be tolerant of her partners? Accept the necessity of her total involvement for the next three weeks?

Her fingers trembled as she brushed them through her damp curls, dark eyes wide and questioning. Could he fall in love with her at sea level? And if he did, could he appreciate all her career meant to her?

If she could tolerate Brutus, she could learn to love cats, she thought as she tripped over his snoozing bulk at the side of her bed. Or at least try. Would that make a difference? she wondered.

Mind hazy with mental and emotional fatigue, Blair slid into bed, buried her face in her pillow and gave herself up to exhaustion.

The next morning, a deep-throated bark brought her abruptly awake. "Brutus, quiet!" Groggy, she raised herself on an elbow as an insistent knocking sounded on one of the doors in the kitchen. "Coming!" she called as she threw aside the covers and reached for her robe. A glance at her clock made her groan. It couldn't be after nine, not when she had so much to do....

She sped through the living room and hall, swung open the door to her workshop and grinned weakly as she met the inquisitive blue eyes of her friend Selena, an attractive, dark-haired woman in the middle stages of pregnancy. "Hi," Blair said, then yawned. "I guess I overslept. Come on in."

Selena looked skeptical as her gaze shifted to the huge black beast leaning against Blair's side. Selena's hand went instinctively to her thickened waistline beneath her potter's apron. "Is it safe?"

Blair laughed. "He takes getting used to, doesn't he? Say hello to Brutus. He's built like a tank but as friendly as a two-year-old."

"Meaning he bites when provoked," Selena responded dryly, edging behind the safety of a wicker chair. "This is a surprise in more ways than one. I thought you hated dogs."

Blair's eyes became guarded. "I do."

"So? Why, and especially *how* did this come about, then?"

"I'm returning him to a...friend."

Selena's attributes included a healthily lusty mind, and it leaped to an enlightening conclusion. "And the owner's a man, right?" A wide grin spread over her glowing features. "Well, I'll be the mother of twins—heaven forbid!" Her eyes narrowed in shrewd speculation. "I don't know what went on up in those wild and wooly mountains of yours, but it must have been sudden and pretty darned serious."

"As crazy as it sounds, you're right on both counts." Blair sighed, giving up on any pretense otherwise. There weren't many personal secrets not openly shared among her close-knit partners. "In fact, it's a little unnerving," she said, then let Brutus out for a quick run.

"Jumping off the deep end always is," Selena chortled, "but it sure keeps the corpuscles alert! Don't expect me to sympathize, either. It's about time you started to really live again, sweetie. Wait till everyone hears—"

"Selena! Keep it under your hat for a while, will you?" Blair pleaded. "He...that is, I'm not sure..."

"Ha! Doesn't sound like it to me," Selena scoffed with her wide, engaging grin. "But okay. I won't say anything. By the way—" her tone grew brisk "—Toddy Baldwin called. Said he has some terrific lithographs we can have for the show—*if* you catch him fast. He's leaving this after noon for L.A. I told him you'd get back to him within half an hour—" she glanced at her watch "—ten minutes ago."

This was a coup! The man was good. Blair's mind cleared of everything else. "Great! Fill me in while I'm dressing, will you? Who's downstairs?" She whirled for her bedroom

"Everyone." Selena trailed her down the hall. "The place is jumping with human striving and sweat of brow. Listen." She watched as Blair pulled a cool cotton shirtwaist dress out of her closet and searched for matching sandals. "We're concerned about your projects. Will you have time to finish them up?"

"Three soft sculptures are ready," Blair answered as she sped for the bathroom. "Which leaves five in various stages, including one stained glass, which I'll finish if it kills me." She knew it meant eighteen-hour days, but it couldn't be helped. Her—the gallery's—reputation was on the line, she thought as she ran a quick brush through her hair. "Ready,"

Blair added, coming into her kitchen. "Oops, I forgot Brutus." She laughed as Selena sought the safety of the other door as the dog burst in from outside, tail flailing in his exuberance.

"Behave while I'm gone," she instructed him. "And stay out of my bed." She shut the door on his woebegone face and met her partner's speculative grin.

"Umm. One wonders if that applies to its master as well," Selena drawled.

"One may wonder all one wants to." Blair grinned back as she turned to head downstairs. But her steps slowed almost immediately, face registering surprise. "Hey, what happened?"

"Another delivery," Selena supplied, eyeing the jungle of boxes in their path. "And if memory serves, we should get a couple more by tomorrow. Who knows where we're going to put it all?"

Storage space had always been a problem. With the gallery's growth matching a need for supplies, the situation threatened to get out of hand. Blair counted a dozen cartons piled on and around the stands, bookcases and screens she used in changing the look of the gallery, some of which had overflowed into her own work area. "We'll use my living room if we have to. After the show we'll give it serious thought. Come on. I've got six minutes to reach Toddy, and I need those lithographs."

But as she followed Selena down the wide set of stairs, Blair's frown vanished. The sounds, sights and scents of the working gallery enveloped her. Sunshine spilled over the flower-filled front courtyard to flood light through the solid bank of windows. Colors and textures glowed in warm invitation from walls and floor displays. Hidden speakers provided a background of mellow rock for the muted roar of Georgio's glass furnace behind its glass and brick enclosure, the soft hiss of Steven's torch as he bent over an intricate piece of jewelry, the scrape of Shag's chisel as it bit into wood. The pungent odor of shaved cedar, faint traces of sulfur from an antiquing compound and a hint of turpentine and oil from Felicity's and Barney's canvases mixed with the lemon smell of freshly polished wood.

Blair could feel a vibrancy in the air, and her steps slowed as she threaded her way toward her back office, calling greetings to all her partners as she glanced around. The Adlib Collection was a living entity and until a short time ago had been the sum total of her existence. The pulsating life around her made her smile. *This* gallery was a far cry from the hushed and hallowed museums of Dominic's experience. How could he *not* be enthused?

Please let him be, she prayed silently, filled with a pressing need to reach him, to let him know she was home.

Selena's voice cut into her thoughts. "The number's there on your desk."

"What? Oh, Toddy's." Blair changed mental gears quickly as she dropped into her chair, ignoring the wry amusement on her partner's face. Concentrating, she dialed the artist's number.

"Well?" Selena asked minutes later.

Blair's smile was pleased as she hung up. "We have our pick of several, provided I go right now."

"Great! That's a start."

"Let's hope it's a harbinger of things to come!" Blair jumped to her feet and dug in her purse for her keys. "If I get any calls, tell them I'll be back in a couple of hours."

"Not if it's your arrogant ex, I won't," Selena stated firmly. "He'd be over like a shot, and I don't want my day ruined."

Blair halted in the doorway. "Oh, gosh. You mean Greg's been calling?"

"Regular as clockwork. He was 'not pleased' you'd skipped out of town. And less so when none of us would give him a clue where."

"Not that it would have done him any good, which was part of the objective," Blair replied grimly. "I wish I could keep it that way."

"Easy." Selena grinned. "You're not back yet."

"Good idea." Blast the man. For the life of her, Blair couldn't figure out what he wanted. But once this crisis was over, she was going to deal with him in no uncertain terms. "I'll see you later." With a sense of urgency, she sped for her car.

During the rest of the day and all the next, her personal life was barely her own as that same sense of urgency nipped at her heels. Sporadic, unsuccessful attempts to reach Dominic had to be interspersed amid the bedlam of nailing down available artisans with available, acceptable pieces. She no longer cared what concept; her creative "theme" had long gone up in smoke. She had *walls* to fill.

And a heart to still, she groaned as Dominic failed to answer yet again. Where in the world could he be at ten o'clock on a Friday night?

Afraid she might not like the answer, Blair hung up and turned to find Brutus looking at her with hungry eyes. His chin lay in his empty bowl, and his woof of hope reminded her that neither of them had eaten. A quick glance in her refrigerator was equally depressing. Which meant a trip to the store despite the late hour.

Leaving a disgruntled dog behind, Blair headed for an all-night supermarket, her mind less on milk, eggs and dog food than on Dominic's whereabouts . . . and particularly on his feelings toward her. Was he having second thoughts? Half fretting, half praying that tiredness was distorting her thinking, Blair swung her car back into its parking spot.

She grabbed her groceries, slid out of the car, and dashed up the stairs and nearly jumped out of her skin as a dark shape loomed out of the shadows.

"So you're finally here," a male voice said.

Though she was caught on the edge of fear, her heart soared with joy. "Dominic!" It was all she got out before she was swept into powerful arms, bag and all. There go the eggs! she thought before the impact of his mouth on hers robbed her of reason. The rich taste of him, the heady reality of his huge beautiful body straining against hers, shot incredible bliss through her heart. A sound of elation sprang from the back of her throat, and as if afraid he'd hurt her, Dominic loosened his arms.

His strong, sensitive hands moved to frame her face as he lifted his head, and his intent gaze locked with hers, eyes connecting, absorbing, asking momentous questions neither could put into words. "Hello, love," Dominic finally managed, his voice low and husky and edged with relief. "Thank God you're home safe and sound."

The tension in his hands spread warmth to her knees, and Blair laughed, a shaky sound overpowered by frenzied barking and a loud thud as Brutus hit the inside of her door.

"Damn," Dom rasped. "We'd better let him out before he breaks it down."

The dog wasn't the only impatient one. Blair couldn't get her key into the lock fast enough. She had just enough sense left to step out of the way as Brutus lunged for his master. Sidestepping the clamorous reunion, she flicked on the lights. With barely controlled actions, she emptied her sack, tossing the eggs and milk in the refrigerator without checking their condition, then bent to fill the dog's bowl, carrying out mundane tasks, filling the time until she could touch him . . . really touch him. She slipped out of her raincoat, dropped it over the back of her chair, then ran a trembling hand through the damp tangle of her curls before she turned, heart pounding, to look at him.

Though Dominic's hands were stroking the dog, his eyes were on her. "Was the trip back okay?"

"Fine." He looked gorgeous! she thought.

"When did you get back?"

"Two days ago."

"Two days!" A succinct word had Brutus dropping front paws to the floor as Dom straightened, eyes narrowing. "Why didn't you call me?"

"I did," Blair answered softly as her hand moved to the scalloped neckline of her cream dress. "You...weren't home."

"Oh, love. You should have called the clinic."

"I tried. Once." She frowned slightly, remembering it clearly in the chaos of the last forty-eight hours. "It must have been after hours."

Dominic groaned. "And I didn't have the recorder on. Damn." He exhaled deeply. "It's my fault." His eyes grew serious as he stepped closer, hands curving over her small shoulders. "I've been working my tail off to free up this weekend." His voice dropped to that determined rumble she remembered. "If you weren't home by tomorrow at noon, I was going to go back up to get you."

"You were?" she whispered, her heart in her eyes.

"Don't look at me like that. My control's just about shot as it is," Dom moaned. His fingers bit into her soft curves. "Do you have any idea of how much I missed you?"

"Not unless you show me," Blair murmured, raising her hands to his chest.

Dominic's growl came from his soul. "Tell me you want what I want, love. Please."

Blair felt dizzy with need. "You, only you." She rose on her toes to brush her mouth against his. "Hurry."

Powerful arms swept across her back and behind her knees as he lifted her high against his chest. The soft hem of her dress swirled to midthigh, and his eyes darkened dangerously. "Where?"

Brutus woofed with interest, and Dom spared him a quick glance. "Stay!" he commanded, then turned his smoldering gaze back to her. "Where?" he repeated hoarsely.

"Through the hall and as far as you can go," Blair managed faintly. Her eyes had found the rapid pulse in the strong column of his neck. It betrayed the thunderous beating of his heart, and she swallowed anxiously as he carried her through her living room. The rain-washed scent of him, the thought of the salty taste of his skin, created a hollowness in her stomach as he unerringly found her bedroom. He had the eyes of a cat.

"Nice," he murmured as he set her on her feet by the side of her bed. But his eyes, narrowed with barely concealed passion, were on her, and she didn't think he was talking about her apartment.

"I'm glad you like it," she whispered, her heart in her voice. With a growl of impatience Dominic peeled off his jacket and T-shirt.

At the same time, she kicked off her low-heeled sandals, her actions barely controlled like the wild rush of her senses. In the faint light from the kitchen, she saw his bronzed naked body straighten, heard the harsh intake of his breath as she dropped her dress to the floor and loosened the catch of her bra.

"Let me." With a whispered command, he came to her, skimming the straps down her arms. Then he went to one knee. With warm, unsteady fingers he slid the wisp of her panties down her smooth legs. For an instant, she stood passive, nails cutting into her palms as her heart slammed in her chest. His uneven breath shivering over her abdomen was her undoing.

With a sob, she ran her hands over the broad ridges of his shoulders and wrapped them around his dark head, urging his mouth to her breasts. Blindly, he closed his hot mouth over one, then the other, drawing their full, aching torment into the sweet succor of lips, tongue, teeth. His hands moved slowly up her legs, his palms and fingers exploring the small curves of her lower body, her soft round hips, until they found the juncture of her thighs. Fire flared through her and she lost control of her knees, and as she buckled he caught her and lifted her onto the bed.

He followed her down, covering her mouth, her body, with his, tongue and tormenting fingers seeking and claiming her innermost heat. Her hands flowed up his back as she strained against him, hot and hungry and aching for the raw hard power of his masculinity. "Dominic, please," she begged.

"Blair..." His voice shook as badly as his hands. With a primitive sound of agony, he took her. And with fierce, urgent, exquisitely timed torture, he brought her to the brink of madness. One last, shattering thrust toppled them both into explosive oblivion.

Time dissolved, fragmented into a thousand prisms of images implanted in her mind and seen through the tears of her completion. She lay spent, still gently trapped in the heat of his body as she savored the lingering scent of their passion, the ripe taste of him.

At last, somehow finding incentive, she moved her hands over his slick back and felt the steady rise and fall of his breathing quicken again as he groaned, lifting his head from her shoulder. "Forgive me, love. You can't be comfortable. Let me—"

She shifted a little and she stopped him with a small sound of protest. "Don't," she murmured. "Stay."

"Oh, Blair. Do you know what you do to me? How perfect you are?" he said softly.

"No more than you," she mouthed against his lips, then teased him with the tip of her tongue until he deepened the kiss. His hands began another symphony of exploration, and her eyes widened as she felt him stir, then grow strong and solid within her. "Dominic...?"

"What you have before you, madam," he said, chuckling low in his throat, "is a modern miracle of motivation. Care to see how it works?"

Laughter rippled through her voice. "I wouldn't miss it for the world."

It proved to be a long, complicated, deliciously decadent night.

They overslept, so in the morning, getting showered and dressed and throwing together a quick breakfast while staying out of each other's way took on overtones of a Marx Brothers skit.

In spite of her hurry, Blair made herself sit and took nervous gulps of her coffee as Dom wolfed down scrambled eggs and toast. Watching his face, she explained the gallery's predicament. To her intense relief, the only expression she saw in his eyes was understanding.

"That's tough, sweetheart," he said sympathetically. "How's it coming? Making progress?"

"Some." She leaned toward him, her forehead creasing with a distasteful decision. "Dom, I don't think you realize what this means. The next couple of weeks are going to be frantic for me. I . . . think maybe it's best if we—"

"If we what?" Warned by her voice, he laid his fork on the edge of his plate, gray eyes sobering as he saw her troubled frown.

"Don't see each other until the show opens." Her words more or less ran together. She caught her breath as Dominic rose to his feet, rescued the cup from her unsteady hands and pulled her up into his arms, his face—that formidable chin—set in determined lines.

"No," he said. It was flat-out refusal. "Don't even think it."

Beneath her hands, she felt the beat of his heart through his thin shirt, yet she forced her chin up, remembering the demands she faced. "But—"

"Just a minute, love," Dom broke in quietly. "Let me finish. I know what this means to you. I admire your determination to pull it off successfully, and I have a pretty good idea of the pace you're going to have to set in order to do it.

But—'' a strong streak of persistence smoldered in the depths of his eyes ''—that doesn't mean we can't see each other. You have to sleep once in a while.''

"And you'll be around when I do, I suppose," Blair supplied dryly. Just the thought of it weakened her will. "Fat chance of sleep *that* means."

"Think of it, love," he growled seductively. "I could fix some dinner, scrub your back, give you a massage . . ."

Linked fully to the persuasive lines of his body, Blair suffered an agony of indecision. "A massage?" she repeated faintly.

"Uh-huh." He grinned down at her. "Masters's strokes of manual dexterity—any night you're free. What do you say?"

Before she could answer, he lowered his head and kissed her, following up his argument with a most convincing display of logic.

He was right, Blair thought, sighing as a wave of raw need coursed through her body. She'd never last two weeks without him. "Okay, you win," she said when she could. Rumpled and thoroughly kissed, she glowed from the heated "discussion." "Dom," she said impulsively, "let me show you my work. Take a look at the gallery." It was more important than ever that she share that segment of her life with him.

Dominic glanced at his watch and said something short under his breath. "I can't, love. I have less than thirty minutes to get home, change, and be at the clinic. Later tonight? A private showing, maybe?"

In her head Blair went over her day's schedule, ruthlessly crossed off the last three items and smiled. "Sold to the man with lipstick on his collar."

He glanced down at his shirt and cocked a lazy eyebrow. "That's nothing. You should see my chest." With a smirk he was gone, leaving Blair in a state of helpless, pink-cheeked laughter.

* * *

"I've been led down the garden path, Ms. Mackenzie."
Dominic's deep voice, pitched slightly above the noise
around them, held mock overtones of accusation. "This
isn't a gallery; it's a three-ring circus."

Blair's laugh rose over the mellow music on the radio
flowing full volume from hidden speakers. So far, so good.
Dom's disappointment over a "private" showing was either
well-hidden or nonexistent. "What do you think of the
performers?" she added, no longer worried in the least.

"I can safely say—" Dom grinned down at her, his eyes
dancing "—they're like no artists I've ever met before."

"Is that good or bad?"

"*Definitely* an improvement. They, this place, are wild."
He glanced at all the activity generated by six people in six
separate throes of creativity. "Is this what goes on during
the day?"

"More or less. It's more noisy and frantic tonight because of the show, of course. Normally, two hours of clas-
sical music is a Saturday-night ritual and our collective way
of winding down for the weekend. Although," she added,
letting him know what he might be in for, "there are times
when we've wound *up*—straight through Sunday."

"I can believe it," Dominic commented dryly. "I get the
impression they're ready for anything."

"Selena said the same thing about you." Blair slanted him
a dark-eyed look.

"Smart lady." His own look deepened, and her eyes fell.
"Dom, I—"

"Have to get back to work yourself," he finished, squar-
ing his broad shoulders. "I don't like it, but I understand.
However—" his mouth grew firm as he glanced at his watch
"—I'll be back later on. There's no way you and I are going
to sleep apart tonight, Blair."

She hesitated, then shrugged and smiled. Who was she
kidding? "I wouldn't dream of it," she answered softly as

he zipped up his jacket, then couldn't resist asking, "What are you going to do in the meantime?"

"What choice do I have?" He quirked an eyebrow and flattened his tone. "In lieu of a certain accessible substitute, I'm going back to the clinic to hug a cat!"

Her laughter was cut off as she was swept into his arms and kissed in no uncertain terms. "Artists," he said short but explosive moments later, "aren't the only ones who can make a statement." His eyes crinkled as hoots of encouragement came from all corners of the gallery. "I think they get the picture."

Hot tamales! Blair grasped at coherent thought as he jauntily saluted and left. They'd have to be blind if they didn't!

Thirteen

***

Sweet, sweet heaven, Blair thought as she dashed through the following days, juggling the different dimensions of her life. This relationship was going to work!

Dominic, "art skeptic *extraordinaire*," had become intrigued with the gallery and her partners. Whenever he could, he'd adjusted his schedule to hers, and as she worked on her own projects to a point where she could quit for the night, she was peripherally aware of him prowling around, asking questions or lending a hand, determined to entrench himself in that segment of her life . . . as well as her bed.

She might not be getting much sleep, she thought, laughing inwardly, but as the date of the opening approached, Blair's energy level soared. She thrived on challenge. And— mind, hands and heart full—paid only scant attention when Maggie called, mentioning in passing that she was more concerned than usual over her eccentric son's behavior.

Bringing his patients home? Disappearing at odd times during the night? "Poor Maggie," Blair murmured sympathetically as she raced off on the heels of a hot tip about a well-stocked sculptor. Once the show was launched, she'd see to it they got together for lunch. Meanwhile, she was up to her ears in work.

And up to certain other heady activities as well, Blair mused one morning as she wove her way through the cluttered balcony and sailed downstairs. The full skirt of her thin cotton dress swished against her legs. Last night's glow was still reflected in her eyes, with her thoughts focused less on the urgencies of the day than on the ones Dominic had repeatedly created and equally satisfied until just before dawn. The man certainly had stamina!

Actually, she wasn't doing so badly herself. Blair's grin spread from ear to ear.

"Good grief, I'm turning green!"

"Selena!" Blair plowed to a halt as her partner popped into view and leaned dramatically against the archway of the potting studio. As her friend's words registered, she took a quick step forward. "Are you all right?"

"Oh, sure." Selena waved an expressive hand. "The last I heard, envy doesn't kill. *Must* you look so all-fired satisfied?"

Full of well-being, with parts of her body still memory-locked with Dominic's touch, Blair kept her answer to a slow, cocky grin, and Selena groaned, rolling her eyes heavenward. "Spare me the lascivious details. From the feel of it, this kid's all ears, and I don't want him totally corrupted before he's even born!"

"I wouldn't dream of it," Blair assured her as solemnly as her laughter allowed. "What are you doing here so early?"

"Approaching the moment of truth."

Unloading the kiln, Blair's interest sharpened. "Greenware or glazed?" she asked, hoping it was the latter.

"Finished product, chum." Selena straightened, momentarily all business. "If nothing disastrous happened, there's twelve pieces of pretty good stuff in there."

"Terrific!" Blair could have hugged her. "I've got my fingers crossed. And if everyone else is doing as well, we just might be in fairly good shape."

"Hey, confine your worries to the artists at large," Selena soothed her trailing Blair into her office. "Thanks to that gorgeous man of yours, the Ad Lib crew stands a damn good chance of being decently represented."

"Dom?" Blair turned from the filing cabinet. "What do you mean?"

"You really haven't noticed?" Selena's eyes widened, then she laughed, her tone turning droll. "Come to think of it, if Dominic was wrinkling *my* sheets, I'd be lucky to focus beyond the bedpost myself. Honey," she crowed, eyes dancing as Blair blushed, "look around. The windows and patio are clean, the extra spotlights are hung, the wine's ordered—"

"Wait a minute!" Blair cut her off. "You mean *Dom...*"

"He most certainly did, bless his magnanimous heart. For which, I might add, we're all eternally grateful. Instead of sweating over the mundane, we get to sweat over our art. It's taken a load off everyone's back." She grinned. "Especially yours, in case you hadn't noticed."

Blair frowned. "I hadn't," she said slowly, not pleased with herself because of it. She was also not all that thrilled with Dominic. She was—figuratively, at least—in charge around here, and he hadn't said a word, much less asked her consent. In typical Masters fashion—as he had up in the mountains whether hauling wine and brandy impossible distances, climbing glaciers for ice, or plowing determinedly into her tent to keep nightmares at bay—when he made up his mind to do something, he did it.

Memory made Blair's resentment soften, and she shook her head, beginning to feel both relieved and grateful. By going straight down her list, he'd been of incalculable help. It was only his methods she questioned. Her mouth began to curve. They were, she decided, going to have a serious talk—after she'd thanked him. Thoroughly. An anticipatory smile grew.

"That's more like it," Selena chortled. "If I remember correctly, you *wanted* him interested, right?"

"Yes, but not *this* interested," Blair commented dryly. "I'm warning you, without a firm hand, the next thing we know, he'll be running this place."

"Oh, glory!" Selena's face lit up. "Can I help wrestle him for control?"

In concert, two sets of eyes dropped to her overabundant waistline, and both women broke up into laughter. "Shame on you, Selena. You're a happily married woman."

"More's the pity," her unrepentant partner said with a sigh. "You get to have all the fun."

"Don't I just," Blair answered in total truth.

Selena's groan was cut short as the phone rang. "I'll get it," she offered, plunking herself down at the desk. "It gives me an excuse to sit."

With a quick glance at the clock, Blair buried her nose in the files, tuning out the conversation as she mentally went over her day's itinerary. Darn. She'd be lucky if she didn't meet herself coming and going.

She extracted a sheaf of consignment contracts, tucked them into a folder, grabbed her purse and turned to leave, only to pause as she caught the sour look on Selena's face. Blair winced as the receiver was slammed back on its hook. "Good heavens, who was *that*?"

"Bea. Your charming ex-in-law." Eyes wide, she slapped her palm against her forehead. "You don't suppose...? No. It's too bizarre."

"What are you talking about?" Blair asked, feeling some of her exuberance drain away. Blast it. The day, which had started off so shiningly, was beginning to tarnish. She had

neither the time nor the interest to deal with the Deadly Duo
and said so pithily as she dug for her car keys.

But Selena was sunk in thought. "Think about it, chum.
She's been calling; he's been calling. Could it be they believe you could be talked into coming back?"

"*What?* Don't be ridiculous! That's too crazy to even
contemplate."

"Don't be surprised," Selena called as Blair stalked out
of the office, dismissing the whole thing from her mind.

The only thing that *would* surprise her, she thought later
after a long, less-than-productive day, was if she made it to
bed before she fell asleep.

Which was not a mood made in heaven for the chaos she
found going on in her kitchen.

As she opened her door, Blair staggered under the triple
assault of Brutus's wild doggy greeting, her counters buried under more groceries than she bought in a month and
Dominic bared to the waist, grinning like a Roman con-
queror.

"What—?" was as far as she got before she was swung
high in his arms, whirled around, skirt flying, and kissed till
her mind spun.

"You taste good enough to eat," he groaned when he finally let her stand on her feet.

Speaking of eating, Blair thought dizzily, still reeling from
the taste of him, there was something she'd been going to
ask. At a sudden crash both of them spun around to find
Brutus with his paws on the counter, a bunch of broccoli in
his mouth, and an uh-oh-I've-been-caught look in his eye.

As Dominic separated beast from broccoli—which Blair
didn't like anyway—she feasted her eyes on the play of
muscles on a bronzed rippling back. Heat rose up and into
her pores, coming, it eventually dawned on her, from the
steamy kiss as much as from the oven.

She blinked, wrinkling her nose. Roasting turkey? On a
hot August night? "Heaven help us," she said, watching as

he tossed chewed greenery into the garbage and turned around. "The man's gone crazy. What is all this?"

His eyes danced. "A bit of foresight mixed with epicurean aptitude, my love." He grinned, encircled her with his strong arms and pulled her close. "Not to mention stocking the fort and the fridge for a siege. I promised you dinner, remember?"

"Yes, but—"

"What's almost as good as hot—" he kissed her on the nose "—succulent—" his mouth curved softly against hers "—singularly seasoned—" he murmured low as his tongue slipped past her lips, tasted and withdrew "—white breast of...turkey?"

Breast? she thought dizzily as hers collided with his. Oh. Turkey. "W-what?"

"Leftovers." The lines of his mouth quirked as he shifted his hands to her shoulders. "Lots of leftovers, including salads, vegetables—"

"Dominic, stop! I don't need—"

"Word is that you do. Besides, your cupboards are bare as a baby's backside. Consider." One dark eyebrow lifted to make his point. "You have a hell-on-wheels week coming up, and I don't want to be tied to the kitty hot line for the next couple of nights worrying that you're skinnying down to a shadow. You're to take the time to eat. As of right now," he intoned, glancing at the clock, "you have just enough time for a shower before the *pièce de résistance* is served."

"But—"

"Scram, ma'am," he ordered, overriding her protest as intractable hands turned her toward the hall. "Your master chef's on the verge of producing a gastronomical extravaganza that's better eaten hot the first time around."

Her saints be praised. He was taking over a large chunk of not only responsibilities in the gallery but now her personal life as well. As much as she loved him, things were—

Dominic was, Blair amended, mentally digging in her heels—pushing her a little too far too fast. She spun back to look at him as an accumulation of his actions came together in her head and spilled off her tongue. "Don't misunderstand me," she concluded a little breathlessly. "I love you for even thinking of helping out. It's...wonderful you're so interested, Dom. But you've been taking a lot of my obligations out of my hands without even asking. That's the part I don't think I like."

Slotted spoon in hand, eyes suspiciously solemn, he managed to look both contrite and innocent of all charges. "Don't let it bother you, my own. Overlook the methods and concentrate on the results."

Blair arched a brow warily. "What results?"

"More time to spend with me." He grinned disarmingly. "And lumpy gravy if you don't quit distracting the cook."

"Maybe you should be distracted," she said, trying to keep a firm stand. "It's something I think we need to discuss."

"Discussion," Dom said as the look in his eyes turned wicked, "isn't exactly what I had in mind. We're talking seduction of the senses here, Ms. Mackenzie. And I promise you, before the night's over, I intend to cater to more than one of yours. Which shall we start on first?"

"Do...I have a choice?" she asked seriously.

"Not much."

"Oh." She paused, then her mouth curved. "In *that* case—"

It was as far as he allowed her to get.

"So if anyone's hungry," Blair addressed the room at large as their strategy meeting broke up, "you know where to come. What do I *do* with someone like him?" She'd meant it as a rhetorical question but was bombarded with answers from all sides.

"Give him to me!" Selena roared as the rest of her partners laughed.

"Right! Relax and enjoy it."

"Are you so far gone you have to ask?"

"Trade him in and you're a goner!"

"Hey, hog-tie him, Mackenzie. He's giving the male population a heck of a good name."

"That's right. If he doesn't have 'conquer 'em with kindness' down to a science. I *do* admire his style."

"Hold it! Whose side are all of you on?" Blair protested, gathering coffee cups.

"Ours," they teased her mercilessly. "And yours," each added later in his or her own way as she was hugged, slapped on the back and left with the feeling she was on her own as far as Dom's bulldozing tactics were concerned.

Her brief experience with Greg, she admitted freely as she slipped her thin nightgown over her head, had strung a streak of caution through her psyche. Yet the feeling that Dominic's full-throttled thoughtfulness, if unchecked, could command as much control over her life as had her ex-husband's selfishness was pure nonsense. How could one compare near perfection with the machinations of an egotistic toad?

As a result of the brevity of their "discussion" last night, Dom might not have been set entirely straight. But, she concluded with a confident smile as she settled into bed, if his huge helping hand threatened to get carried away again, all she had to do was say no.

A supposition, Blair found less than thirty-six hours later, to have as many holes as Brutus had fleas. With Saturday's opening galloping closer, she'd been on the run since dawn, collecting last-minute artwork. So she was grimy, disgruntled and distinctly displeased to discover said dog flaked out on her bed and Dominic deep in her closet.

"What in the world?"

"Found it!" His dark head followed the broad planes of his body as Dom straightened, tossed a dark lock of hair off his tanned forehead, flashed her a full-powered smile and settled her suitcase near the foot of her spread. "And you, darlin', are just in time."

"For what?" she asked, almost certain, just from the look in his eyes, she wasn't going to like it.

"We're packing you up, love. Bag and baggage. You're moving in with me."

Thunderstruck, Blair sagged against the wall. Her mouth opened and closed as her brain finally connected. "Have you gone completely out of your mind?" she whispered.

"If I have," he stated impatiently, "that makes two of us. Have you taken a look at this place lately?"

"My apartment? What are you talking about? Of course I have."

"Then the only one slightly unhinged is you. I had to snake my way in here and shift boxes of supplies the hell and gone before I could even *get* to your bed."

"So what? It's a temporary—"

"So's the mess in the living room, I suppose."

"Mess!" Blair's voice shrieked like a noonday whistle. "You're calling the whole Ad Lib show a mess?"

"Is that what it is?" He grinned, unrepentant, then shrugged. "It still doesn't make the place habitable. What's it doing all piled in there, anyway?"

It was none of his arrogant business! Blair seethed like a ripe volcano. She'd known all along he was a masterful man. But *never* had she bargained on this blatant, overbearing rerun of male domination. Who did he think he was! "Put it back!"

"What, the boxes?"

Had she really thought he was perceptive? Ha! He was as dense as a doorknob. "The suitcase! *Put it back!*" The force of her words could have split boulders.

"Blair—"

"Don't you 'Blair' me, *Mr.* Masters. And get that in-fested animal off my bed!"

"Oh, now, wait a minute." His voice lost some of its silkiness. "I just gave him a bath."

"In my tub?" She dug her fingernails into her palms, which ached to have both his and his itchy animal's hides. "Out! Both of you, out!" For Pete's sake, lending a hand was one thing; taking over, another. Blair put her foot down. Hard.

Which snapped both man and dog to attention. Tail between legs, Brutus slid off the bed and beat a hasty retreat. But Dominic stood his ground, gray eyes thoughtful but, she wasn't surprised to see, as resolute as ever.

"Blair," his voice soothed her, inviting reason, "take a minute to think about it. What, after all, is the problem?" He moved closer and she stiffened. "We know we love each other. It's going to happen sooner or later. The gallery needs all this space for storage—"

Blair cut him off. "Did you ask what *I* wanted? I will make my own decision, when or *if*, Dominic Masters. Now, put it back."

"That's just it," he murmured. His hands reached out, claimed and cupped her furious face and turned it up to his, searching her eyes with warm, increasing urgency. "I *want* you to make a decision, Blair. Move in with me. Now. Let me give you my heart, my hearth, my home. I swear I won't crowd you. You can come and go as you please, as long as you come back to me when you can."

Backed to the wall, her heart melting all over her anger, Blair hesitated, trapped between captivation and capitula-tion. "Your timing is terrible," she finally whispered. How she loved this huge, impossible man. How could she say no?

"So you always tell me." His off-center smile held a hint of soberness as his coaxing hands slid to her shoulders, spreading heat through her chest and down to her knees.

"But don't let it rob us, Blair. We've found what we've both been searching for. Help me grab it before it gets away."

His words up in the mountains rang in her mind like a clarion call. And the last of her misgivings dissolved. Time, she swore silently, would *not* rob him again.

With a smile of her own, with just enough sense left to promise, "Oh, Dominic, yes...but *after* the opening, please." Blair stepped into his arms and was swept into the brushfire of his passion. Please, she prayed, may I never taste the ashes.

"Who? Oh, Maggie!" Blair heaved a sigh of relief, switched the receiver to her other ear and sank down on a chair, as delighted to hear her friend's voice as she was to take a much-needed breather.

"How are you, my dear? Up to your ears?"

Blair grinned. "More or less, but it's coming together beautifully." Craning her neck, she glanced into her living room, enormously pleased with the results of her preliminary groupings. Piecing together colors, textures, designs, into composite, complementary clusters was as much a thrill to her as the financial success of a show. "I can't wait for you to see it."

"That's one of the reasons I called," Maggie answered, her own voice reflecting excitement. "Need any last-minute help?"

"No, thank heaven...and thank you for asking. Oh, Maggie, I never thought we'd make it, but we're so on schedule, we're moving everything downstairs tonight. Can you stop by? I guarantee you a cup of coffee that'll make your hair stand on end and a personal grand tour."

Maggie laughed. "As irresistible as that sounds, I believe I'll pass. To tell you the truth, between trying to guess what the Sam Hill Doc's up to and the zany interest rates sending my business soaring, my hair stands on end enough as it is! But I promise I'll be there tomorrow night as soon as the doors open.''

"It wouldn't be the same if you weren't," Blair said with real feeling. "You've never missed one yet."

"Nor do I intend to." Maggie's voice grew stout. "Is that young man of yours going to be there?" she added almost on the same breath.

"I'm not sure," Blair answered airily, unable to resist springing Dominic on her as a surprise. "We'll have to see."

"Now, Blair. I've been counting on giving him the royal once-over. I have a *very* experienced eye."

"Don't I know it." Blair chuckled. "But I think you'll like what you see. The man's gorgeous."

"Sounds like you're taken, all right. As long as you're happy, that's all that matters. Now, I'd better let you get back to work. Oh. It may not be entirely apropos, but...break a leg!"

Show biz was show biz, no matter which kind, Blair mused the next night as the last of her opening-night jitters disappeared in the overcrowded gallery. If sheer numbers and enthusiastic comments intermingled with the discreet ring of the cash register were any criteria, their performance rated rave reviews.

She stood near the bottom of the stairs like a small flame, her soft apricot dress highlighting both the flush of accomplishment on her face and the sheen of mahogany curls that enhanced the darkness of her eyes. Only one thing marred her total happiness...Dominic's puzzling absence.

"Ah, *there* you are." Selena broke through the crowd, a glass in each hand. "Some mob scene, huh? Here. Drink up." She pushed the wine into Blair's hand. "That and the news that your stained glass masterpiece just sold should help put some sparkle back into your eyes."

"Where do you suppose he could be, Selena?" Blair's worried gaze searched the room again. "It's not like him not to be front and center." Maggie had come, lingered long, and gone, as had the first-, second- and third-wave arrivals.

"Look," Selena's voice grew practical. "If you're that concerned, run upstairs and give him a call. Maybe he had an emergency or something."

"Or something." Blair's mind refused to go further. "I think I will."

"Don't hurry back," Selena advised her as Blair turned away. "This place will start thinning out pretty soon. You've had a hell of a week, so let the rest of us close, okay? We can rehash tomorrow."

But Blair hardly heard. Her heart raced ahead of her less-than-sedate retreat up the stairs, her hand clammy with nerves on the doorknob. She stepped into her kitchen and nearly jumped out of her sandals as she was trapped in familiar arms. "Dominic!" She gave a startled shriek.

"It's about time you got here," he growled, laughing low in her ear. "Congratulations, darling. It seems the show's a success."

"How would you know, you beast?" Blair's fear turned to puzzlement as she tried to wiggle out of his grasp. "Where have you been? Why weren't you downstairs?" His hands, she rapidly discovered, had no intention of yielding.

"For several valid reasons," he answered, then groaned, gray eyes losing some of their calmness as she moved against him. "First, this was your evening to savor a personal triumph. Second, cultured or uncultured, I hate crowds. And third—" his mouth curved in lazy assurance "—after the last several weeks of catch-as-catch-can, I've grown unwilling to share you with anyone for some time to come."

"Is that a fact?" Blair whispered, registering his words in the dark regions of her body. She slid her hands slowly upward, over the fine broadcloth of his shirt, trembling with the memory of raw power and muscle and sleek warm skin that could thrust her straight over the rim of reality. Her breath caught in her throat as she was swung high in the air.

"Fact," he assured her succinctly as he carried her toward the bedroom.

"Uh, Dominic?"

"Umm?"

"Are we . . . er, sharing the bed?"

His smile was slow, dazzling and sexy as all get-out. "That's the general idea, my love. Any objections?"

"Well . . . yes, actually."

His smile, like his step, faltered. "Why?"

She linked an arm around his neck, tilted her head to look at him and kept her mouth solemn. "I only sleep with one male at a time."

His eyes narrowed dangerously, then lit as light dawned. He cursed softly, grinned and kissed her. Hard. "Brutus, you teasing wench, is out of sight, out of mind and out of contention. The only animal in your bed is going to be me."

"Really?" Blair's smile was serene as she stroked idle fingers around the strong column of his neck and down to the first button on his shirt. "You know, that's interesting," she said as fabric separated. "The very first time I saw you, I mistook you for a bear."

He dropped her none too gently on the bed. "Is that so? Well, if bear is what you want—" his voice roughened in promise as he shed shirt and tie "—bare is what you get."

He was demanding. And hungry. And she couldn't get lost in him quickly enough.

The night became a private celebration.

Fourteen

Congratulatory calls might be balm to her professional soul, but the phone itself, Blair decided as it rang for the umpteenth time, was going to drive her crazy!

Tucking the tail of her scoop-necked blouse into the waistband of her wrap-around skirt, she sped, barefoot, for the kitchen, grinning as she passed her bathroom, where, loud and lusty, Dominic sang slightly off-key in the shower. What a voice!

What a *man*, she amended, skin deliciously shivery as she snatched the receiver in the middle of a persistent ring. "Yes? Good morning."

"It's about time, Blair. Where in the hell have you been?"

She came down to earth with a thump. Who else but the gracious Greg. Leopards did not change their spots, she thought. Neither did polecats. Or certain ex-husbands. "None of your business, actually," she answered more pleasantly than he deserved. "What is it you want?"

"To see you. To talk to you. Dammit, Blair, you've been giving me the runaround for weeks. Stay put. I'm coming over."

"No!"

"Blair—"

"Greg, I said no." It was time to end this nonsense. "Pay close attention. I—"

In true Nicholson form, he ignored her. Voice confident, with just a hint of cajolery, he plowed over her objections, intent on getting his message across. "Okay, if you won't see me, then at least listen. Six years as a starving artist is enough for anyone, Blair. Even you. What I'm offering you is your old job back, no strings attached. And a raise in salary. How does that sound?" he said smugly.

"What salary? I never saw a dime!" Selena's sixth sense never fails, Blair thought. I should have remembered that. "And the answer is no! I'm not interested on any level, at any price. I happen to be satisfied, solvent—" which, after last night, happened to be true "—and seriously involved with someone," she couldn't help adding.

"What do you mean involved? Who with?"

"You mean," she said sweetly, "who's *lucky* enough to get me? None of your business, Greg."

"Are you telling me you're getting married?" he demanded, sounding as if hell had just frozen over.

Oh, gosh. Blair glanced toward the bathroom, where Dom's voice and the water still roared. Although he'd asked her to share his heart and his home, Dominic hadn't mentioned marriage. All she could do was hope. "I'm thinking about it," she answered truthfully enough.

"Dammit, Blair. Yes or no?"

"Read it in the newspaper, Nicholson," she said shortly, and hung up.

Greg all but forgotten, Blair sank into a white wicker chair, toes curling against the sun-splashed tile floor. Why *hadn't* Dominic asked her to marry him? Didn't he *want* a permanent commitment? From the moment they'd met, every word he'd said, every instinct she had, said yes. But . . . what if she was wrong?

"Hey, bright eyes, what's up?" Huge and imposing, the man in question loomed large in the doorway, wearing nothing but water-glistened skin and a skimpy towel.

Blair's heart turned over with love. She stood and stepped into his arms. "The sun, among other things," she said softly, running hungry hands around his waist as she turned her face up to be kissed.

His smoky gray eyes flared with a hot, bright light as one huge hand gathered her close. The other he raised to brush unsteady fingertips over her cheek, down the slim line of her throat to rest on the soft contour of her breast. "Ah, Blair . . ."

They groaned as the telephone pealed.

"Don't answer it," he murmured huskily.

"Okay," she agreed, more than happy to tune out the rest of the world. She felt his pause through her pores. Then he raised his head, eyes laughing and incredulous as the telephone sounded again. "You'd actually do that?"

Blair grinned. "Uh-huh."

"Well, I'll be. You're one in a million."

"My priorities are right on target—" her eyes dropped significantly "—which is more than I can say for your towel," she said, then scowled fiercely as the phone sounded again. "Oh, blast it," Blair muttered, then gave up, lifted the offending instrument and heard the voice of her ex-mother-in-law. "Hello, Bea." She sighed sardonically. "What a surprise." Dominic's response was more emphatic.

Choking back a laugh, Blair waggled her eyebrows in agreement, listened politely for all of sixty seconds, then cut in on the diatribe beleaguering her ear. "Talk to your son, Bea. I gave him my answer not five minutes ago."

She severed the connection, checked for a dial tone, then laid the receiver down on the counter. "We," she said, "are alone at last."

"Until someone bangs on the damned door," he answered dryly.

He'd readjusted his towel, she was sorry to see, and his eyes were more watchful than wicked. The sight depressed her, and she mumbled succinctly under her breath.

A corner of Dominic's mouth twitched, and his eyes crinkled. "Do you mind my asking what that was about?"

"No, of course not." Blair moved away restlessly, turned, braced her elbows behind her on the countertop and looked him straight in the eye. "Greg, my ex-husband—"

Dominic's hand sliced through the air. "I know who he is."

"Called while you were in the shower. *That*—" she gestured with a disdainful tilt of her head "—was guess-who."

"They wanted—?"

"Me! Can you believe it?" Her dark eyes flashed. "Oh, they phrased it in two distinct, arrogant styles, but the message was the same." She shook her head, still amazed. "Talk about exquisite timing! Only hours after the biggest coup of my career." Her voice grew mockingly pompous as she intoned, "Am I not through wasting my time and ready—properly subdued, of course—to come back?"

"Hold it right there!" Dominic's eyes darkened dangerously. "What do you mean come back?"

"Greg offered me my old job."

"Ah. At the paper." His broad shoulders relaxed.

Blair snorted. "If he'd suggested anything else, I'd have crawled through the phone lines and bitten him."

"I believe it." Dom grinned. "And you said?"

She waved an expressive hand. "What else can one do but laugh? Although," she said, scowling, "when I was forced to live in that house under both their thumbs, that sanctimonious superiority wasn't funny."

It was not, Blair decided as they finished breakfast, the most propitious time for Dominic to suggest she meet his mother.

"What? Are you crazy?" The man boggled her mind!

"Then I should blend right in." He chuckled. "You and that bunch downstairs aren't exactly Sane City."

"Dom! Be serious!"

"Oh, I am." He stepped closer, cupping his hands on her small shoulders. "You're moving in with me, remember? It might be...diplomatic to meet Peg first, don't you think?"

For the life of her, she couldn't see why. "But—"

"No buts, my love." His hands slid coaxingly to hers. He raised them to his lips, kissed each palm till she melted, then pressed them against his chest. "Come on. What do you say?"

Well, she thought dizzily, at least he'd *asked* this time. Besides, the thud of his heart through her fingertips was an aphrodisiac. Still high on a wave of professional and personal euphoria, she started to laugh. It was just bizarre enough to be funny. "All right," she said. "When?"

"How about this morning?"

Blair gulped. "Oh, gosh."

"Don't worry. It'll be fine." The knuckles of one large hand brushed over her cheek, then stilled as he took a deep breath. "Honey, I think I should..." he began, met the hesitant look in her eyes, and, whatever it was, changed his mind. "You're going to love each other," he said softly.

Blair made a face as she made a beeline for her bedroom. From firsthand experience, she doubted it very much. "You are *flowing* with confidence," she muttered as she dressed with care. And almost believed it as she swished the slim hem of her amethyst coatdress into her car with a jaunty air.

She was practicing her warmest attitude when Dom suddenly pulled over to a curb. Surprised, Blair glanced out the window. They'd traveled only two blocks. "What did we forget?" she teased him. But her smile faded rapidly as she caught the expression on his face. "What is it? What's wrong?"

"Everything," he groaned. Draping his wrists over the steering wheel, he bowed his head for a moment, then twisted to look at her, eyes—for pity's sake—looking determined yet almost...anguished. "I can't do it," he rasped harshly.

Blair's stomach fell through her open-toed shoes. Can't do what? she thought in a sudden panic. Love her? Have her move in? Introduce her to his mother? *Can't what?* Her face paled as all her old insecurities came back. "I don't understand," she managed in a tight voice. "What are you talking about?"

With an air of dismay, she watched him stab frustrated fingers through his hair as he inhaled, held a deep lungful of air, then let it slowly escape. "Sweetheart," he began, visibly choosing each word with aching care, "I can't let you go into this meeting blind after all."

"Blind? Dominic, don't dance around," she ordered. "What is it you're trying to say?"

He cursed softly under his breath as his eyes met hers. "You're not going to like it. But I swear my motives were pure. Will you promise to listen and not prejudge either me or the situation?"

That didn't sound too bad so far, although Blair's dark eyes remained wary and her palms grew damp. "All right," she answered with relative composure. "Tell me."

Reaching over, he captured her hand and gently sandwiched it between the two of his. "Blair, believe me. I knew my—what can most charitably be called blundering, full steam ahead and without asking—has nearly blown things between us more than once lately."

"Oh, Dom, I—"

"Don't say anything yet," he advised her. His mouth thinned wryly. "Not until you've heard the rest."

His deep voice lowered. "Oh, Blair. You jumped into my heart for all time the moment you leaped over the campfire and into my arms. That's why I pushed you so hard and so fast. I had real hope you'd feel the same. Heaven knows the chemistry was there, the laughter.... But when you told me about the trauma you'd gone through in your marriage, with Bea's stiletto tongue, you tossed me on the horns of a hell of a dilemma. At that point," he said with a sigh, "I made a decision. A wrong one, maybe, but it's the reason I kept quiet until now. I didn't want to lose you. And I didn't want to prejudice you against Peg."

Silence hung in the car like a breathless spectator as his disquieted gray gaze met hers. "In a manner of speaking, she lives with me, Blair." He cleared the hoarseness from his voice. "With . . . er, us, that is, once you've moved in."

"What!"

The depth of his deception in that whispered word made Dominic wince. His hands came together like a clamp, crushing her fingers before she could pull them away. "It isn't the same, Blair, I swear. Trust me."

"Trust you?" she gasped. Her skin felt hot, her ears rang, and her voice rose. *"Trust* you? When, knowing my feelings, you *kept* this from me?"

"Knowing your feelings is precisely why I did it." His deep masculine voice rang with sincerity. "The setup's not anything like what you're thinking," he assured her. "And wait till you meet her. Peg is—"

"Don't tell me—Peg Perfect!" Blair exploded bitterly. "Where have I heard *that* before! Let go of my hand. *Let go!"*

Reluctantly, still arguing his case, Dominic complied.

Free of his touch, Blair closed her mind and her ears to the forceful flow of his words as he drove home the rest of his explanations. How could he! she fumed. Anger swirled through her breast like a riptide. She surged out of the car to the sidewalk, slammed the door on his "Listen to me, dammit!" and stormed off, breaking into a fleet-footed run as she heard him shout behind her. Ducking in some doors and out of others, she dodged into a side street, seeking a deep hole to hide in. If she weren't so livid, she'd break into a thousand pieces.

But that would come later.

Right now she was too busy swearing. He'd done it to her again!

She could still hear his explanations. But did she care that Peg was a "marvel"? And fiercely independent? Heck no. Or that, as part owner, she inhabited the *other* half of a sprawling complex? It was under the same roof, wasn't it? And did she care? You bet she cared. How did she *know* that their personal privacy—so earnestly guaranteed as she'd scrambled out of the car—was as unassailable as he claimed?

But the real conflict, she knew, had nothing to do with Dominic's one and only relative. At issue was his damnable determination—*in spite of his promises*—to make decisions without her consent. *That* flaw was fatal.

But so was a broken heart.

"What I need," Blair muttered to a lamppost, "is a good, stiff drink."

Losing track of time and locale, Blair wandered through Edmonds's cluster of back streets, keeping a leery lookout around her for a low-slung gray car. Easy to spot, she thought, rubbing salt in the wound, since the color matched his quicksilver eyes.

Eventually the pain of her feet in her spike-heeled sandals gained her more immediate attention. It took her a moment to orient herself, then, aching inside and out, she limped down the hilly sidewalk in search of somewhere dark and dim.

The quiet restaurant on a side street she finally chose was as dark as a cave to her sun-blind eyes. She was thankful the decor supplied low lighting close to the floor, but how was she supposed to find the bar?

Squinting, she took a step forward and tripped over a pair of well-shod feet. "Oh! I beg your pardon...."

"Blair? Is that you?" A familiar face loomed out of the darkness.

"Maggie! What are *you* doing here!"

The older woman laughed. "I was about to ask the same question." Her smile faded. "You look upset. My dear, is anything wrong?"

Now that her vision had adjusted, Blair could see. Appearing more than a little haggard herself, Maggie was gazing at her with obvious concern. Blair's eyes filled. "My feet hurt," she said with some truth.

"What a coincidence. So do mine. Let's find a place to sit. Can you see where you're going? I don't know why these places have to ape the Stone Ages," she complained lightly as she half led, half dragged Blair to an isolated table. "Ah, here we are. Now, what will you have?"

"Oh, I . . ." Blair hadn't thought that far.

The decision was taken out of her hands. In the following hour she was plied with hot soup, several glasses of Chablis, and such a steady stream of manufactured nonsense that, disillusioned or not, even Blair had to smile faintly.

"That's better." Maggie looked exhausted but pleased. "Now. Tell me what's wrong. Dollars to doughnuts it's got something to do with a man, right?"

"Not 'man, right.' Wrong *man*." Under the influence of a fourth glass of wine, Blair's eyes looked a little glazed as her normal reticence slipped. "I . . . have to tell you, my friend," she hiccupped solemnly, "I'm no longer taken, but *took*."

Maggie was splendidly furious. "Men can be such unpredictable beasts!" Beneath the crown of silver hair, her blue eyes flashed. "I should know, having been married to two myself. I just don't understand them. Take Doc, for instance—"

"Maggie, forgive me," Blair interrupted her. "I don't mean to be rude, but *you* take him. I . . . right now, I . . ."

Brimming with remorse, Maggie immediately changed tactics. "Of course," she said stoutly. "What we need is a fattening dessert. Over which—" she caught a hovering waiter's eye "—we shall wish *all* men to perdition. Who needs them, anyway?"

"I do," Blair admitted bleakly, breaking the silence a few moments later as she dug a spoon into the nutty confection. She raised stricken eyes. "But how can I live with a man so set on making every decision? If only Dominic would *ask*! I'm supposed to live with his mother. Can you believe it? His *mother*! —*Maggie!*" she yelped as her friend turned purple. "She's choking! Help me, someone!" Blair's chair went flying as she leaped around the table, pounded the gasping woman on the back, then staggered as she was pushed aside.

"Water!" someone yelled.

"Grab her around the middle!"

Half the restaurant's clients had converged, shoving Blair out of the immediate picture. But before Blair could gain her balance or catch her own breath, Maggie, with the strangest look on her face and a brief apology tossed over her shoulder, was gone, leaving Blair nonplussed, frantically searching for her shoes . . . and stuck with the bill.

"Is your friend going to be all right?" the anxious manager asked.

How would *she* know? Blair thought in bewilderment as she fumbled for her credit card. It had all happened so fast. But if mobility meant anything, probably so. Who would dream Maggie could recover and move with such speed?

She shook her head, and was instantly sorry as everything spun a little off center. Oh, help. She needed fresh air!

But out on the sunny sidewalk, she faced another dilemma. She couldn't go home. Suppose Dominic was there. She needed time and a place to lick her wounds, to sort out her feelings.

The hoot of a ferry's signal drew her down to the shoreline. A round-trip cross-sound ride would give her two hours, but all she had in her purse was her credit card. Instead, she cut over into the waterfront park, slipped off her high heels and trudged past the crowd of sun-worshippers, strewn out like so much flotsam on the sandy beach, until she found a deserted spot at the north end. Sinking down on a log, she stared out over the open water, letting the serenity seep into her soul. Somewhere in her wanderings, she had lost her anger. But not the pain.

Nor, she discovered as the day passed in a blur, the nagging voice of reason. Of all the impressions that had been swirling around in her head, two salient points kept surfacing. It was about time she paid them some heed.

She was strong enough to hold her own—with anyone, in any situation. And she loved Dominic to distraction.

Could she swallow her pride and go back? And if she didn't, a voice in her head accused her, wasn't she still a victim of her first marriage? Wasn't Dom? Which in the long run made Greg and Bea the winners.

Never! she swore, daring a passing seagull to disagree as she surged to her feet. *She* was in charge of her destiny. And what she wanted—dominating, demanding, or not, with a dreadnought of a mother or not—was Dom.

And she—as she had the car door—had slammed his love in his face.

Please, she prayed as she ran pell-mell down the beach in the gathering gloom, let me find him. Let me explain....

Four uphill blocks later, her feet and her breath a shambles, Blair staggered to the foot of her stairs and nearly tripped over a back blob blocking the bottom step. "Brutus!"

Lungs robbed of air, she sank to her knees. The animal's chest was heaving as hard as hers. His ears drooped, his unsightly tongue hung out of the side of his mouth, and his breath was as doggy as ever. He was gorgeous.

For wherever Brutus was, could Dominic be far away? Throwing her arms around the black brute's panting body, she gave him a quick hug. "Come on. Upstairs. Let's find him, boy!"

But the dog refused to budge, choosing instead to slobber affection all over her hand, whine with excitement and gaze at her with expectant eyes. "Come on," she urged him as she stood. "Move!"

Obligingly, he rolled over, pinned her feet to the ground and stuck his paws in the air. Metal clanked on the pavement, and for the first time, Blair noticed a thick metal tube attached to his collar.

Brutus whined again. If he'd opened his mouth and spoke English, the message couldn't be clearer.

Not questioning her logic, she snapped it loose and gave it a twist. The cylinder fell open in her hands. For a second she just stared at the rolled piece of paper, not sure what to think. But the dog lumbered to his feet, barked as if she'd done something clever and sank back on his haunches. Obviously, she was doing something right.

Heart beginning to pound, Blair unrolled the paper, skimmed quickly over its contents, then, hands trembling, read it again.

TO WHOM IT MAY CONCERN

I, Dominic Masters, being of sound mind (a debatable point, since I freely admit to being fathoms deep and crazy in love), do solemnly swear, promise and take an oath in blood to Blair Mackenzie that from this day forward, I shall never—repeat, NEVER—make a decision concerning us both without her express consent. In other words, *talk it over first*! How about it, Blair? Am I forgiven?

Dom

Wonder of wonders! Not only had Dominic put his vocal promises in writing; he'd had them notarized! She was in love with a man who was as off the wall as they came, she thought, laughing. No false pride there. "You," she crooned, dropping a kiss square between Brutus's big brown eyes, "are a very clever dog. And you have a *marvelous* master!"

Spinning around, she took the stairs two at a time. As she reached her door, she heard the phone ringing inside, and her heart leaped. She dropped her keys twice before she got the right one, then came close to turning an ankle as she dashed inside.

"Don't hang up, don't hang up," she muttered fiercely as she reached out and nearly yanked the receiver off the wall. "Dom? Oh, Dom, I'm sor—"

"Blair? This is Maggie. Thank *heaven* you're home! My dear, I'm in a terrible mess. You've got to help me."

Thrown off balance, Blair went momentarily blank. "Maggie? Wait a minute. Slow down," she exclaimed. "What's the matter?"

"Help me, Blair. Please! I'm—"

Whatever she was trying to say grew garbled, and Blair clutched the phone to her ear. "I can't understand you. What's wrong? Where are you?" she asked, growing alarmed. Maggie sounded frantic. Behind her, Brutus started to howl, and the hair on the back of her neck stood up.

"The restaurant. The same one. Oh, Blair," Maggie's voice seemed to die on the vine. "Come and get me," she whispered. "Please."

"I will! I am! I'm coming! I—"

But Blair was talking to dead air.

Fifteen

The place was as dark as she remembered, and jam-packed to boot. Breathless, a little panicked by now, and fearing God knew what, Blair ruthlessly threw her one hundred pounds into the mob scene, searching everywhere for her friend's face.

Coming up empty after a frenzied but fine-tooth combing through the bar and dining room, she caught sight of a row of booths in the back. Turning, she wedged her way in that direction. They were her last hope.

And the last high-backed booth was where she found her.

"Maggie!" Blair gasped in relief. She rushed forward as, blue eyes brimming with unshed tears, the older woman slid to her feet and stepped to meet her. "I got here as fast as I could. Are you all right?"

"Blair." Maggie all but enveloped her in a smothering hug. "Oh, my dear," she exclaimed as a tremulous smile spread over her face. "I hope I didn't alarm you. But I just couldn't resist—"

"What she means," said a deep, familiar voice at Blair's ear, "is that she has an irresistible penchant for heavy drama."

Startled, Blair spun around. "Dominic! What...what are *you* doing here?"

"My dearest darling," he said solemnly, gray eyes warm with unmistakable laughter, "although she doesn't deserve it after the stunt she just pulled, I'd like you to meet my mother."

The trio was kicked out of the bar at closing, and Margaret Masters Cappelini, hiccupping her blessing, was tenderly placed in a taxi.

"Good night, Maggie," Blair murmured against the woman's soft cheek.

"You *do* forgive me, my dear, don't you?"

"In the interest of our future relationship," Blair teased, "can I do anything else?"

"Well, yes, now that you ask." Maggie's smile grew positively beatific. "Have a baby, darling. I'm *dying* to be a grandmother."

Blair's splutter was drowned by Dominic's rumbling laughter. "I did warn you, didn't I? If she could, she'd have a high hand in that, too. Good night, Peg," he added firmly. "Expect us when you see us."

She placed a detaining hand on his arm, blue eyes shrewd, bright and as intractable as his. "You marry that girl and bring her home soon, Doc. You hear me?"

"As soon as Blair gives the word. Meanwhile—" he gave her a quick hug "—I'll do my best to advance the cause." His grin was so earthy and wicked that Maggie started to laugh and was still chuckling as he clicked the cab door shut.

"What do you say, love?" he asked, wrapping his great arms around Blair as the taxi sped away. "Shall we talk it over?"

"Talk!" Blair placed her hands on his chest and raised what she hoped were indignant eyes. "My dear Mr. Masters, haven't you something better to do with your time?"

His groan made them both weak in the knees. "Your place or mine?" he asked, giving her the choice.

"Mine," she answered, smiling to herself. "It's closer. Although," she cautioned him as she was swept down the street, "I should warn you. Those boxes are still piled all over the place." She cocked her head and flashed him a sexy, challenging look. "Do you think you can still find the bed?"

"Watch me," he growled against her willing mouth.

And watch him she did, with eyes as dark and as dramatic as the rippling movements of his matchless body. When at last he turned to her, naked and splendid and powerfully aroused, she stepped straight into his arms.

"Easy, tiger," he murmured. He moved his lips tantalizingly slowly over the planes of her face. His hands cupped, then lifted the swelling heaviness of her breasts. "I promise you, this is going to last not just tonight, but for a lifetime, Blair." He whispered the words against her nipples, and as they pearled, he stroked them with his tongue to stark, agonizing need.

He closed his lips over her breast, drawing it deeply into the warm, suckling cauldron of his mouth, and Blair moaned as she wrapped her legs around his waist. Her fingertips buried themselves in the rich texture of his hair, holding him close and closer still as his long, sensitive fingers found the raw quickening flower of her femininity and coaxed it to full bloom.

"Ah, Dom!" she cried out, caught in the warm flood of her feelings. "Please, love..."

"Soon, my own, soon," he told her hoarsely. With a slow, powerful twist of his body, he turned and lowered them both to the bed. The spread under her back held only a moment's coolness before she was lost in the scent, the taste, the touch of him as his lips covered hers. His tongue began a renewed deliberate, demanding, provocative mating dance with hers as his hands moved to cosset her breasts, still moist from his mouth.

The fluid muscles of his broad back flexed beneath her fingertips, and she arched into him, wanting the full weight of him on and in her ready body. "Dominic," she gasped softly as his palm slid downward, building unbearable tension as he pressed against her inner thighs, "please, now." Restraint all but vanished, she brought her hand around his hip and clasped him against her abdomen. With a swift stab of satisfaction, she felt him grow taut.

"Oh, love," he rasped. And his need as great as hers, he eased himself forward so that his full, smooth hardness penetrated to the core of her being. Raising her lips to his, she caught the scent of her perfume on his face, tasted the faint saltiness of her skin in his mouth as their tongues tangled again in a lover's duet. In and out and around, she challenged him, promising everything, daring him in teasing withdrawal until he growled in the back of his throat. His hands clamped to her waist and he thrust again, again, and yet again, until he struck the match to her inner fuse and together they exploded.

"Blair. My own," he murmured brokenly into her hair as his hands held her, smoothing over the damp silken skin of her back. "I love you, my darling. Everything that I am is yours."

Her mouth, she discovered, was open, her teeth bared against the splendor of his shoulder. Her breasts were seared to the heat of his chest, the awesome strength that was his was buried to the hilt. And still it wasn't enough. If she could have found a way, she'd have fused herself to his body. How could she *ever* have walked away from this man? He was hers, as she was his, and she'd fight to the death to keep him. "As I love you, Dominic," she said urgently. "With all my heart."

"Blair, look at me," he whispered roughly. This time she raised her head, her dark eyes meeting the unarguable, ruthless determination in his. "Promises be damned.

You...are...mine. Do you understand? *Forever* mine," he intoned with rough finality. "I will never let you go."

"Try it, and I'll sic Maggie onto you," she swore just as seriously as she linked her hands behind his head.

She felt as much as heard the rumble of laughter start low in his chest. "I'd throw up my hands in surrender, but I don't want to let you go."

"In case you haven't noticed," she said, smiling serenely, "I'm clinging to you like a limpet."

"That, my dark-eyed beauty, is perfectly all right with me."

"So I'm beginning to notice." With smug satisfaction, she snuggled closer, tilted her head and made a poor attempt to be serious. "What should we do about it, Masters?"

He narrowed his eyes in thought. "There are...several possibilities." His hands began to smooth over her skin in a deliberate foray. "Call a halt and discuss it, for one. Until we reach...um, a compromise. Or—"

"But I like it like this," she protested, wriggling a little for emphasis. She loved being linked to him in this elemental way. Loved the flare of arousal fracturing his concentration, the sensual curve of his mouth, the deliciously decadent depth of his reborn desire. And it showed in her eyes.

"Who said anything about shifting?" he growled as he eased himself down to pin her more neatly beneath his big body. "Does that suit your fancy more, Ms. Mackenzie?"

"My fancies and a few fantasies, thank you," she whispered. "Oh, Dom, I'm sorry I didn't listen to you this morning. I—"

"Hush, darlin'," he admonished her roughly, soothing the mahogany tangle of curls from her small face. "I'm the one who was at fault and deserved far rougher treatment than you gave. Although—" his eyes darkened "—I have to admit I had a few bad hours when I couldn't find you and seriously doubted you'd listen to me at that point if I did." He grinned slowly. "That was when I decided to give you something—the letter—to hold over my head. At least Brutus stood a chance of getting a foot in the door."

Frowning, he eased himself away, settled on his side and pulled her close in his arms. "I didn't know whether you'd read it or even believe it, Blair. But I meant every word." His arms tightened fractionally as warmth deepened his voice. "From this moment on, this is an equal-opportunity relationship."

It was all she'd asked. "Oh, Dom," she whispered. Needing more contact, Blair raised her hand to trace loving fingers along the line of his jaw. "Before I got home, I'd thought it all through and was just as desperate to reach you." She paused and started to laugh. "I wish you could have seen your mother's face when she put two and two together at the restaurant. Did she tell you she came close to causing a riot?"

"It was nothing compared to what happened when she caught up to me." He grinned, flexing his massive shoulder. "I haven't had a dressing-down like that since she caught me playing doctor with the girl next door."

"Dominic! You didn't!"

"Hey, I was seven and a half at the time," he defended himself with a boyish grin. "Not only that, but I'd had to bribe the little terror with a month's allowance, and all I got for my pains was a half splint on one of her fingers."

"Ah," she said understandingly, trying hard to keep a straight face. "No wonder you switched to animals. It was cheaper."

"And easier on my backside. Peg figured if I got too...bold, they'd bite." He paused, then smiled. "She was right."

"But it didn't stop you."

"I don't discourage easily."

How well she knew! Blair smiled at the thought of his young and earnest dedication, and lamented those years she hadn't known him. No wonder Maggie had nicknamed him "Doc." But... "Why do you call her Peg, Dom?"

"It's a derivative of Margaret." His face sobered slightly. "It was my father's private name for her. After he died, I...didn't want her to lose that fragment of their life together as well."

Blair's heart melted all over her rib cage. "Oh, Dominic," she whispered with a catch in her voice, "you're a very special man."

He gathered her close and rolled her small body on top of his, hands framing her face so their gazes could lock. "Special enough not just to move in with but to marry, Blair?"

The growing heat of his skin, the thudding beat of his heart against her breast, matched hers. "Yes. Oh, yes."

His hands moved restlessly. "Soon," he stated.

She raised her eyes, then captured his face in her hands. "Dominic, love," she said distinctly, "are you asking or telling?"

Gray eyes crinkled with a twist of wry humor. "Old habits," he said, dropping an apologetic kiss on the end of her nose. "Okay, my own. When?"

Sighing in satisfaction, she kissed him back...not so quickly. "Tomorrow, if you'd like," she answered in all seriousness.

"Oh, sweetheart, if I could change the requirements, I would," he groaned, low and deep. "How about Saturday?"

"Six whole days," she said mournfully.

"Interminable." He gave her a sly look. "But it does have its bright side."

Blair arched skeptical brows. "Oh, yes?"

"The news will keep Peg at bay. As much as I love her, when it comes to matchmaking, the door's slammed on subtlety. Which is why I made sure she didn't have a clue about what I was up to until I had enough time to convince you you wanted what I wanted...and as badly."

Blair touched her fingertips to his mouth. "Well, you succeeded." She grinned and shook her head. "Oh, Dom, you should have heard her. You were driving her crazy, staying out until all hours of the night—"

"How else was I going to see you?"

"Bringing your patients home..."

He shrugged. "In lieu of a certain accessible—"

"And so on and so forth," she finished, remembering his lament about having to hug a cat. "I had you pictured as not only a workaholic lunatic but one who shamefully neglected his mother as well."

"Instead," he said as seriously as he could, "I'm as domesticated as they come." He amended, "Or I will be when I get you in my own bed."

"At least Maggie will know where you are nights."

His smile flowed clear to the corners of his sexy mouth. "If you think that's going to satisfy her, better guess again."

"What else...? Uh-oh." Blair's smile spread. "Shall we?"

"It's up to you." His voice was a study of pious neutrality, but his eyes were alight with quicksilver fire.

"When is Grandparents' Day?"

"I don't know, but we can check the calendar, if that's what you'd like."

"Oh, I'd like," she answered softly, entranced by the idea. "With a little luck, we might get it right the first—" she lowered her head and brushed her mouth against his "—or the second time."

"All it takes is practice," Dominic murmured. Beneath her, his big body moved restlessly. "Trust me."

"For the rest of my life," Blair vowed, and surrendered to the blazing masterstroke of his talented hands.

From his hiding place under the bed, Brutus sighed, closed his eyes, and, well-mannered beast that he was, covered his ears with his paws.

*   *   *   *   *

Silhouette Desire

COMING NEXT MONTH

#373 INTRUSIVE MAN—Lass Small
How could Hannah Calhoun continue to run her boardinghouse with any semblance of sanity when all her paying guests were pushing her into the all-too-willing arms of Officer Maxwell Simmons?

#374 HEART'S DELIGHT—Ashley Summers
Cabe McLain was resigned to a life of single parenthood—but that was before Laura Richards showed him that her childhood friendship had ripened into a woman's love.

#375 A GIFT OF LOVE—Sherryl Woods
Meg Blake had learned early on that most problems were best dealt with alone. Matt Flanagan was the one to show her otherwise—teaching her firsthand the power of love.

#376 SOMETHING IN COMMON—Leslie Davis Guccione
Confirmed bachelor Kevin Branigan, the "cranberry baron" from STILL WATERS (Desire #353), met Erin O'Connor—and more than met his match!

#377 MEET ME AT MIDNIGHT—Christine Flynn
Security agent Matt Killian did things by-the-book. He had no intention of having an unpredictable—and all too attractive—Eden Michaels on his team. But soon Matt found himself throwing caution to the winds.

#378 THE PRIMROSE PATH—Joyce Thies
It took an outrageous scheme from their respective grandparents to find the adventurous hearts beneath banker Clay Chancelor's and CPA Carla Valentine's staid exteriors. Neither imagined that the prize at the end of the chase was love.

He could torment her days with doubts
and her nights with desires that fired her soul.

Ride the Eagle

VITA VENDRESHA

He was everything she ever wanted. But they were opponents in
a labor dispute, each fighting to win. Would she risk her brilliant
career for the promise of love?